THE MYSTERY OF THE BROBDINGNAGIAN BEAST

THE THREE INVESTIGATORS

IN

THE **MYSTERY** OF THE
BROBDINGNAGIAN
BEAST

BY

ELIZABETH ARTHUR
& STEVEN BAUER

BASED ON CHARACTERS
CREATED BY ROBERT ARTHUR

Hollow Tree Press 2025

CONTENTS

1

An Invitation To Trouble

As Pete Crenshaw listened to his mother talking on the landline in the kitchen, he wasn't paying much attention to what she was saying or why his father had called unexpectedly in the first place. Still, she looked a little worried, or maybe just surprised. Was something wrong?

Up until the moment the phone rang, his mother had been sitting at a small oval table, a pale-yellow-covered book open before her. Valeria Crenshaw taught fifth grade at Rocky Beach Elementary, but now that school was out for the summer, she was once again ready to explore her other passions – one of which was alternative spiritual paths.

Although she and Pete's father were both practicing Catholics, she was sort of a free thinker and open to other interpretations of the invisible world. Three antique Chinese coins lay on the oval table with the book. Pete's mother had been consulting the I Ching again.

As for Pete, he had been deep in thought about the day that lay ahead. Well, the afternoon and evening, anyway. It was already almost lunchtime, and after lunch he was planning to bicycle out to the Rocky Beach Animal Rescue Center, where he hoped to become a volunteer.

Just ten days or so before, Pete and his best friends Jupiter Jones and Bob Andrews had freed a great horned owl caught in plastic netting at a recreation park in the town of Auburn, about four hundred miles north of Rocky Beach. They'd been up there in their official capacity as The Three Investigators.

Pete remembered the way Jupiter had cut the netting carefully while Pete held the bird close to his chest. The owl's talons had pierced his leather gloves and cut his wrist. This had hurt a lot – and when the owl was freed, it had tried its best to bite him – but Pete had understood that the owl had just been scared.

When Pete got back home, he'd called the Animal Rescue Center to see if they could use him as a volunteer. The coordinator of volunteer services was a man named Mr. Munson, and Pete had made an appointment to get a tour of the Center at 1:30 this afternoon. Bob had said he'd like to go with him and should be arriving any time.

The only thing was, Mr. Munson had told him that even though Pete was turning fourteen in October, he would still need his parents' permission to volunteer. And it wouldn't be enough to just get his mother or father to sign a permission slip; one of them would have to come to the Rescue Center on his first day there.

Pete's mother couldn't go today, because she had a commitment to do something or other at the church, and his father couldn't go, either. Martín Crenshaw was a set construction supervisor for a major motion picture studio, and right now he was up in Sonoma working on a historical epic called *Bear Valley*, about California in the mid-1800s. Pete didn't know much about it – not even whether it was a Western!

Anyway, it really didn't matter if Pete became official today. Even becoming *unofficial* would be very exciting, he thought – and he hoped the day would prove eventful not only for him, personally, but also for The Three Investigators. This evening, he, Bob, and Jupiter were going to dinner at the house of Isabella Chang, the woman whose ancestor, Li Chang, they'd been researching when they were up in Auburn. In the course of their investigation, they'd found a pouch of gold Li Chang had hidden over a hundred years before, and when a judge had awarded the pouch to Isabella Chang, she'd been so grateful she'd decided to give a portion of the treasure to the boys.

Even now, Pete could hardly believe it. The gold – or the money it was being turned into – would take some time to get processed, but Ms. Chang had asked The Three Investigators to dinner to celebrate in advance. They'd met Ms. Chang at the house of the mystery writer Hector Sebastian but they hadn't been to *her* house yet. It was on the outskirts of Rocky Beach and they'd be able to bicycle there in ten or fifteen minutes.

Rocky Beach was a great town for biking, and since he and the other Three Investigators wouldn't be able to drive in California until they turned sixteen, Pete was glad they all had bikes and could use them to go anywhere local in the meantime. Still, when the reward money *did* come through, he, Bob, and Jupiter had decided to put three-fifths of it into their individual college funds and use the other two-fifths to buy a secondhand car, hire a driver to drive them to their cases, and pay for other firm expenses.

A car of their own! Pete thought.

Of course, for years they'd had the use of a gold-plated Rolls-Royce owned by the local Rent-'n'-Ride — after Jupiter had won it in a contest. It had come with its own British driver, and since Worthington and The Three Investigators had now become friends, their plan was to hire *him* to drive them. For the moment, however, they *had* no car, and they also had no case to solve.

At least, Pete didn't think so.

But as his mother hung up the phone and turned to him, her face was still creased with surprise and a bit of worry.

"Well, the I Ching didn't tell me *that,*" she said. "Not that it ever tells me anything directly. It seems your father is on his way home. Not for long, but still, he'll be here this afternoon. He may even be here in time to drive out to the Rescue Center and sign your permission slip."

Though Pete should have felt happy about that, his mother's expression made *him* worried.

"Has something happened to Dad?" Pete asked.

"No, no," his mother said. "Nothing like that. But it seems there's been some trouble on the set. He'll tell you all about it when he gets here. It doesn't sound that serious, but some protest group called OUTLAW is trying to shut the movie down."

"Shut it down?" Pete said. "Not really!"

"Your father told me the protesters have drawn so much attention that a local news crew showed up yesterday afternoon to film the protest and to interview the director and some of the film's advisers," his mother said. "He thinks the segment may be on at noon, if you want to watch it."

"But it's almost noon now!" Pete said.

"You're right," said his mother. "And that means I've got to go!" She was wearing a brightly-colored peasant blouse and her gold hoop earrings shone in the late morning light as she swept the Chinese coins off the table and put them in a little suede pouch.

"I'm sorry I won't be able to see Bob," she said. "Father Francis wants to talk to me about leading a Bible study for children, and I'm already almost late." She grabbed her shoulder bag, tossed her black curls back, and headed for the door to the garage.

Just then the doorbell rang. "That's Bob," Pete said. "I'll see you later, Mom!" He shot to his feet. When he swung open the door Bob Andrews stood there grinning. He'd carefully tilted his bike against the trunk of a magnolia tree. Bob was careful about everything.

"Hey!" Pete said. "I've been waiting for you. I made us some peanut butter sandwiches and lemonade. But we've got to turn the news on. Some protesters are trying to shut down the movie my father's working on, and there's supposed to be a segment about it on *The News At Noon*."

There was a small 10-inch portable TV on the kitchen counter, and as Pete and Bob settled down with their lunch, Pete grabbed the remote from the table and pushed a button, then tuned in to a local affiliate in Santa Monica. The anchor was a youngish-looking guy with blond hair in a crewcut. The lead story was about the economy, about interest rates and inflation, and as the guy rattled off numbers, Pete grimaced. Maybe he'd understand all this stuff one day, but not today.

The angle changed and the man swiveled in his chair to face the second camera. "In other developments," he said, "the protest group OUTLAW is in the news again. In their latest demonstration, they've moved north to the town of Sonoma where they're trying to shut down a movie being made there. The movie is called *Bear Valley*. It takes place in the mid-1880s and centers on John Frémont, the explorer, naturalist, and politician – and California's first senator. According to OUTLAW – which stands for 'Outing Lawbreakers From Past Centuries' – Frémont is a controversial figure whose history the movie is attempting to whitewash."

As Pete watched the little TV screen, it was suddenly filled with an unruly crowd of several hundred. They held handmade signs with Frémont's name in a circle with a slash across it. Many wore black bandanas over their noses and mouths and they thrust their fists in the air and chanted. Police stood stolidly behind a barricade, their hands clasped behind their backs, but Pete could tell from the way they stood that they were on edge.

The newscaster was back and Pete didn't want to miss a word of what he was saying.

"The film is based on a book by a local historian, Dr. Phillipa Paxton, who teaches at Reedmore College outside of Rocky Beach and is acting as an advisor on the film," he went on.

"Wow!" Bob said. "Maybe my mom knows her!" Bob's mother was an evolutionary biologist who taught at Reedmore.

"Dr. Paxton's book is called *Bear Valley: A Prodigious Destiny*. OUTLAW claims its view of Frémont is uncritical and hagiographic."

Pete looked at Bob quizzically. Bob was a wordsmith and could generally be counted on when Pete needed help.

"*Prodigious* means something that's really big," Bob said. "Enormous. But generally not a physical thing. Like you'd say someone had a prodigious talent."

"And hagio – ?" Pete asked.

"I think *hagiographic* means too flattering. That the book turns Frémont into a saint."

Back on screen, the flat-topped anchor went on. "Studio executives are reportedly in a panic, and with his film under threat, Richard Black, the director of *Bear Valley*, has acceded to some of OUTLAW's demands. He is making some changes to the script and he's hired a second advisor, a historian with an opposing view of John Frémont. Here, from the set of *Bear Valley*, is our very own Emilia Cortez with an exclusive interview with historian Daniel Hernández."

The TV screen was filled with a two-shot of a young woman with thick plastic-framed glasses holding a microphone standing opposite a good-looking man with olive skin. Pete thought he was in his late thirties or early forties. He was wearing an expensive dark blue suit that looked as though it reflected light. He stood casually in front of a red brick building Pete assumed must be in downtown Sonoma, and he looked at Emilia Cortez with what seemed to be paternal concern.

"Dr. Hernández," the reporter said, a bit breathlessly. "Thanks *so* much for talking to us today."

"Not at all, Emilia," Hernández said. "I'm always happy to be of help to the press."

"Are you connected to OUTLAW?" Cortez asked. "And if not, how did the director, Mr. Black, choose you?"

"I'm not connected to OUTLAW in any way," Hernández said decisively. "Though I do think they are bringing attention to part of the historical record that often goes unremarked. Richard Black chose me, I believe, because in my book *Manifest Murder: John Frémont and the Taking of the American West* I argue that Frémont was hardly the good guy my esteemed colleague Dr. Paxton makes him out to be."

"So you think the movie should be shut down?" Emilia Cortez asked.

A look of what seemed to be shock crossed Hernández's face and he placed one hand on his heart. "Of course not!" he said. "I say let the two sides argue, and may the best man – I mean person – win."

"Yikes!" Bob said. "What a sleazeball! And what an actor! He ought to be *in* the movie rather than advising about it."

Pete was puzzled. Sure, Hernández was a little full of himself, but this was TV! He wasn't sure why he hadn't felt the same way Bob did. Maybe he wasn't as observant?

The interview was soon over, as was the segment about OUTLAW. Pete glanced at his watch and saw that, if they didn't hurry, he'd be late for his appointment at the Animal Rescue Center. As he quickly cleaned up the kitchen, an old insecurity resurfaced. In the past he'd worried he wasn't really cut out to be an investigator. Jupiter and Bob were naturals, but he had to work at it. All the way to the Rescue Center, he thought about Daniel Hernández and what it was that Bob had found so untrustworthy. He couldn't come up with anything in particular.

The Animal Rescue Center was basically just a converted barn on the outskirts of Rocky Beach, but it sat on two acres of land and had some mature live oaks growing in the areas where the animals were mainly kept. Still, it was a hot June day, and by the time they arrived, Pete and Bob were pretty sweaty. Pete worried that they'd make a bad impression, but since there was nothing he could do about it now, he was happy when Mr. Munson turned out to be a really nice guy.

He had a graying beard and a bit of a pot belly, but his beard was trimmed, his eyes were kind and intelligent, and he seemed to be in very good shape for a man in what Pete thought was probably his early 60s. Soon, he was showing Bob and Pete around.

The Rescue Center had a number of adult owls and hawks and eagles, but it also currently held two red foxes – one of which had an incredibly red face and tail. There were three baby barn owls that had fallen out of a nest. As well, there were striped skunk kits and opossum joeys, coyote pups and bobcat kittens. Pete asked Mr. Munson why so many young animals had shown up all at once.

"It's hard to know for sure," he said. "Their mothers were probably hurt or killed – sometimes by other animals, and sometimes by people. Of course, people *are* animals – and sometimes a lot more ferocious and savage than all the other animals put together. But when they find orphaned babies or injured adults, they often bring them to us. We've even gotten young, orphaned bears. Do you want to hold a baby bobcat?"

"Can I?" asked Pete.

Mr. Munson opened the cage that held two striped kittens, picked one up, and handed it to Pete.

"That's right," he said. "Hold it just like that. You're a natural."

The bobcat did look like a kitten, though larger. She peered up at him, her greenish eyes cautious.

"How old is she?" Pete asked.

"About three months," Mr. Munson said. "She won't reach her full size until she's two, but I think she and her brother ought to be fine if we release them together in about a year."

"Do you really get bears here sometimes?" Pete asked. "I didn't even know there were still bears in California until I went camping in Yosemite. I thought they had all died out." He set the bobcat kitten carefully back into her cage.

"Only the grizzlies," said Mr. Munson. "There hasn't been a wild grizzly in the state in almost a hundred years. Human beings have always wanted to be the biggest and fiercest predators around, and grizzlies are quite dangerous. Luckily, there are still grizzly populations in Canada, Montana, and Wyoming."

"Wyoming?" said Pete. "Bob and I know a mystery writer named Hector Sebastian who's just moved there from Rocky Beach."

He didn't want to sound as if he was bragging – and he also didn't know whether or not Mr. Munson had ever heard of The Three Investigators – but he couldn't stop himself from adding, "Before he moved, Mr. Sebastian used to help us publicize mystery cases we solved. Now Bob is writing up our cases himself."

"Hector Sebastian!" said Mr. Munson. "I've read a couple of his novels. Then you must be two of The Three Investigators! I read in the Rocky Beach *Herald* about that gold you found. That was impressive work."

Pete blushed. He wasn't used to such praise, and he'd been getting quite a lot of it since he, Bob, and Jupe had returned from northern California. He turned his face away from Mr. Munson, but suddenly, from the parking lot, came the screech of tires, and Pete turned to see his father's shiny red pickup come to a stop.

"Wow!" Pete said. "My Dad got here after all!" His sudden appearance seemed to move things along really quickly. In no time, Pete had filled out the formal application, Mr.

Crenshaw had given his consent to let Pete work around "wild and potentially dangerous" animals, and Mr. Munson had walked them to the door of the old barn.

"I think you'll do great," he said to Pete. "Give us a call when you're ready to start."

"I will," said Pete.

The parking lot's heat was like a slap in the face, but Martín Crenshaw didn't seem to notice. Rangy, fit, and muscled, he was wearing a light blue tee shirt, worn Levis, and cowboy boots, and he had a red bandana knotted around his neck. His skin was brown from the sun; he was clean-shaven and his black hair was short on the sides and longer on top.

"Let's go!" he said. "Where are your bikes?" He picked up one and then the other as if they were toys and settled them securely in the truck's bed. Then they all piled into the cab.

"Mom told me you might get here," Pete said as his father pulled out of the parking lot and stepped on the gas. Both windows were wide open and a cooling breeze swept through the cab.

"I was afraid I wouldn't," his father said. "But I made excellent time."

"Mom also said that there was trouble

on the set."

Mr. Crenshaw's face lost its smile.

"We were watching the news," Bob added, "right before we left for the Center. There was a piece about OUTLAW and they interviewed this guy named Daniel Hernández."

Mr. Crenshaw's head swiveled and he stared at Bob, his face grim.

"That son of a – "

Wow! Pete thought. I guess Bob was right!

Mr. Crenshaw took a deep breath and composed himself. "Did the news say what the movie is about?"

"Not really," said Bob. "What *is* it about?"

"This guy named John Frémont and his wife Jessie," Mr. Crenshaw said.

"Yeah," Pete said. "We know. The guy on the news said *that* much."

"Well," his father went on, "the two of them had a place in the Sierras called Bear Valley, but the film centers on the Bear Flag Revolt. You guys must know about that. I hope they're still teaching that in school."

Pete only vaguely remembered it had something to do with the California state flag, but he wasn't surprised when Bob knew everything about it – how before the Mexican-American War really started, some American settlers captured Sonoma, which the Mexicans held, and arrested the officer headquartered in the barracks there.

Bob said, "I think they took a sheet and painted a bear and a star on it with red paint, then hoisted it over the barracks and declared themselves the leaders of the California Republic."

"The first version of it, anyway," Pete's father said. "What ended up getting called the 'Bear Flag Republic' only lasted three-and-a-half weeks."

"So what's the movie about? Is it a war film? Or a Western?" Pete asked. "And what about this trouble? What's been going on?"

Pete's father sighed. "There were rumors almost from the moment we started shooting that OUTLAW was going to show up and protest," he said, "but we didn't pay too much attention. Not at first. But then Richard – Richard Black, the director – kept getting these phone calls and anonymous text messages, some of them pretty ugly and threatening. Plus a bunch of so-called activists started a smear campaign on social media, aimed at the studio heads who, as I'm sure you can guess, are wusses and totally risk-averse."

"Uh-oh," Pete said. "And then OUTLAW *did* show up."

"Boy, did they," Mr. Crenshaw said. "First just a handful, but more and more every day. It seems they have a Facebook page. We've had to hire private security. The Sonoma police can't handle it all by themselves. Some of the actors' trailers have been broken into. Equipment has been stolen – they seem to have hijacked lighting equipment and even an Arri Alexa."

"What's that?" Bob asked.

"An expensive digital movie camera," Mr. Crenshaw said. "Props have gone missing –. I could go on and on. Everyone's on edge. It's a real mess."

"So how did you get away?" Pete asked.

"Richard decided to close down the set for a day or two, to give everyone a breather, and to see if we can regroup and get started again."

"So what's the deal with the Hernández guy?" Bob asked.

"He is one slick character," Mr. Crenshaw said. "And I suspect he's a lot more involved in all the trouble than he's letting on. He's really out to destroy John Frémont's reputation. Can you imagine that? Frémont's been dead for a hundred thirty-five years. Can't you let the dead rest in peace?"

"What did Frémont do that Hernández hates so much?" Bob asked.

"If you want *my* opinion – absolutely nothing!" He shook his head in disgust. "My guess is he's just trying to make a name for himself by raising a stink. He claims that John and Jesse pushed the idea that the west should be part of the United States rather than part of Mexico or Canada. Someone called the idea Manifest Destiny – that's where Hernández got the title of his book.

"According to Phillipa Paxton," Mr. Crenshaw went on, "John Frémont had nothing to do with any of that, but OUTLAW is outraged because it claims American settlers used the idea of Manifest Destiny to justify killing Native Americans. They seem to think that if California had stayed Mexican, the Indians would still own their land. Now why do I doubt that?"

By now, Mr. Crenshaw had reached the residential part of Rocky Beach. Everything seemed quieter, cooler, more peaceful.

"Anyway, Frémont was an interesting character. He was a great explorer. He led three big expeditions through the West – two of them guided by Kit Carson," Pete's father added.

"Kit Carson!" Pete said. "Is he in the movie?"

"I don't think so," Pete's father said. "But if he is, I'm sure Hernández will try to make him look bad too." He pursed his lips as though he had something sour in his mouth. "I don't say this very often, but if Hernández and I had been in high school together, I probably would have punched his lights out."

"Gee," Pete said. "You really must hate the guy. I wish I could do something to help."

The smile returned to Mr. Crenshaw's face. "Here's the thing," he said. "Maybe you can. I thought The Three Investigators might come up with me to Sonoma and do some looking around. Some snooping."

Pete was astounded. "Really?" he said.

"Really," his father said. "I don't know if you'd be interested, but if you are, you wouldn't have to be The Three Investigators. You could just be my son and his friends who are coming to get a look at how a movie is made. Sort of undercover. You could keep an eye on things. See if you notice anything suspicious. What do you think?"

"Are you kidding?" Pete asked. "Bob, are you in?"

"You bet," Bob said. "Of course, we'll have to ask Jupiter – "

"Jupiter will *love* it," Pete said enthusiastically.

"Good," Mr. Crenshaw said. "That's settled. I could really use your help."

Pete's face burned with elation and his heart beat hard in his chest. There was a mystery on the set of *Bear Valley*, and The Three Investigators had been asked to solve it. Who had stolen the equipment and props? Who was breaking into the trailers? Not only was Pete determined to find out who was behind the trouble, but now that he knew that it wasn't just Bob who distrusted Daniel Hernández, he was resolved to look more carefully, to make a study of the man. If there were goods to be gotten, he'd get the goods on Hernández and make his father proud!

Mr. Crenshaw drove more slowly through the leafy sun-dappled streets of the town where Pete had lived his whole life. Rocky Beach had a small-town feel that had made Pete comfortable while he was growing up, but now that he was a teenager, he was ready for the larger world. They dropped Bob and his bike off at the Andrews' house and then drove on, each of them lost in his own thoughts.

The truck passed the Jones Salvage Yard where Jupiter lived with his Aunt Mathilda and his Uncle Titus – and where The Three Investigators had their headquarters in an old mobile home trailer camouflaged behind piles of junk. Pete craned to look in through the wrought-iron entrance gates but no one was out in the yard.

The closer they got to home, the more antsy Pete felt. As they pulled into the driveway, Pete opened the door before the truck had even come to a stop.

"Whoa!" his father said. "Be careful!"

"I'm going to call Jupiter right away!" Pete said. He practically flew up the stairs to the landline in the upstairs hall. He grabbed it and dialed the number of Headquarters, hoping like crazy that Jupiter would be there to hear about OUTLAW, Daniel Hernández, John Frémont, and the Bear Flag Revolt!

The Mystery Begins

About an hour later, Jupiter, his Uncle Titus, and the Jones Salvage Yard's two Norwegian carpenters, Leif and Magnus Haldorsson, were working together to secure a load of reclaimed lumber Jupiter's uncle had just bought. Leif and Magnus were hauling it off the truck, examining each board for the fineness of the grain and the absence of knots, and sorting it into grades. Jupiter and his uncle were stacking the brothers' various grades in piles under the overhang that ran around the inside of the Salvage Yard, at the top of its high wooden fence.

Leif and Magnus had begun working at the Jones Salvage Yard a few months earlier. Though the brothers looked alike − tall, lean, and exceedingly blond − they were quite different in their outlooks. Leif, the elder, had a sunny disposition, while Magnus, three years younger, was generally skeptical and sometimes downright pessimistic.

The brothers seemed to work well together, though − better, Jupiter thought, than he and his uncle did sometimes.

"Jupiter?" Uncle Titus said. "Are you paying attention, or are you thinking again?"

"Both," said Jupiter, walking backwards.

Together, he and his uncle were carrying a stack of five quite heavy boards, with Jupiter trying to keep watch over his shoulder to see where he was going. His uncle was walking too fast, and more than once Jupiter stumbled.

As they neared the fence, Jupiter veered to the right, where the less perfect boards were stacked. He had thought they'd begin a new pile, but evidently his uncle assumed they'd just stack the boards on top of the teetering pile they'd already begun. When he stopped short, the boards slipped from Jupiter's hands.

As they clattered to the ground, his uncle dropped them, too, and they bounced and twisted. Jupiter had to jump out of the way before they caught his shin.

"Whoa," Magnus said. "I was afraid of that. Everyone O.K.?"

"Titus," Leif said. "You were pushing the boy."

"Was I, Jupiter?" Uncle Titus said.

Jupiter didn't want to say anything; he just wanted to get on with the job.

"Maybe *I* should walk backwards," Uncle Titus said.

Leif had a good relationship with Jupiter's uncle and liked to tease him. "You're too old to walk backwards, Titus," he said.

Magnus hit his brother on the arm. "Leif!" he said.

"It's O.K., Magnus," Uncle Titus said. "He's probably right. Want to give it another go, my boy?"

Jupiter nodded, but before they restacked and picked up the boards they'd dropped, he checked with Leif to make sure these were not the finest grade.

"Ja," Leif said. "You were right. You should listen to him, Titus. He's very smart."

"I know how smart he is," his uncle said. "I knew even before *he* did!"

He and Jupiter picked up the boards and started a new pile. As they worked, Jupiter thought about the news Pete had given him when he'd called. He hoped The Three Investigators were really on the trail of a new case. Although Bob had only just finished his report on their last one, Jupiter was eager to get started on something new. During the times he had no puzzle or mystery to solve, he felt a bit slack. The world seemed dim, its colors not so vivid or its sights so interesting. He loved the feeling of being fully engaged by a mystery; he could almost feel his body kick into a higher gear.

He was also eager to cram as many cases as possible into the summer that lay ahead. After high school started in the fall, he and Pete and Bob would have little time to solve mysteries. Though they'd long ago understood that they learned just as much, if not more, from their work with The Three Investigators as they did from their formal schooling, all three of them were headed to college, and Rocky Beach High School was very competitive.

Indeed, unlike a lot of American schools these days, it still *believed* in competition. It believed hard work should be encouraged, and that those who worked harder and did better should be rewarded. During the school year, he and his friends would need to spend most of their time studying. That made it important to take advantage of every day before school started at the end of August. He hoped nothing would get in the way.

Since he didn't know exactly what he meant by that thought – which seemed to come out of nowhere – he set it aside for the moment to think about something else. Jupiter would never have imagined when their last case started that it would end up where it had, but this evening, he, Pete, and Bob would be having dinner with Isabella Chang.

Leif and Magnus unloaded the last of the boards and Jupiter and his uncle carried them to the side of the Salvage Yard.

"That's a good day's work," Uncle Titus said. "Thanks, boys," he called to Leif and Magnus. "And thank you, Jupiter. As a reward, here's a puzzle I made up while we were working."

Uncle Titus was always giving him puzzles to solve; they both loved puzzles. "This one's about a snail," his uncle said. "The poor little guy is stuck at the bottom of a ten foot hole and wants to get out. Each day he manages to climb up four feet, but at night he slides back three. How long until he gets out of that hole?"

Jupiter closed his eyes to visualize the problem. This one was pretty easy, but he had to keep in mind how high the snail got at the end of each day. On day 1, he got to four feet before sliding back; on day 2, he got to five feet; on day 3 to six feet –

"The snail reaches the top," Jupiter said, "on day seven."

"Excellent," Uncle Titus said. He looked

at Jupiter with pride. Jupiter was pleased, no matter how elementary that particular puzzle had been. He was really getting a little old for this, but it made his uncle happy, and it was easy enough to do.

Leif and Magnus were resting in the shade of one of the trees that grew inside the Salvage Yard, and Leif called out to Jupiter.

"About the immigrant's trunk we're making for your friend Mallory MacLeod?" he said.

Ah! thought Jupiter with sudden satisfaction. *That* had been the source of the elusive thought – the one that had seemed to come out of nowhere. When he had hoped that nothing would get in the way of a summer crammed full of cases, what he had meant by the 'nothing' had been a girl with red hair and a Scottish accent.

He had met her in Grass Valley at The Next Chapter Bookstore, but she lived, with her mother, in an apartment in Rocky Beach, and though she wasn't quite Jupiter's friend, he wasn't about to get into a discussion about it with Leif.

"Yes?" he said.

"Magnus and I have finished our sketches and are ready to start building," Leif said. "We have two different designs – one with a flat top and one with a domed one."

"That's great," Jupiter said, "but Bob is the one who'll need to decide which to use. He'll be over later."

Friend or not, Jupiter had to admit that The Three Investigators' last case wouldn't have had a successful conclusion if it hadn't been for Mallory. She was their age and had recently arrived in Rocky Beach, after growing up in Scotland. Her father had died seven or eight months before, and when school was over, her mother had moved the two of them back to the town she was from.

Mallory had stopped by the Salvage Yard one day and had met Pete – and, after that, Bob, in the Rocky Beach Library. Both Bob and Pete had taken a shine to her – especially Bob – but it had been a coincidence that she and The Three Investigators had all ended up in the same bookstore on the same day.

If truth be told, Jupiter had never had much use for girls, and some years back when Bob had met a girl named Liz Logan in the course of the case of the Fiery Eye and had suggested to Jupiter that maybe she could help them with cases sometimes, Jupiter had nixed the idea at once.

But Liz Logan had never actually proved her usefulness as what Pete liked to call a "girl operative," while recently, up in Auburn, Mallory had seen at once that what Jupiter had thought was a Chinese talisman was actually a disguised map – and if she hadn't, The Three Investigators might never have solved the case. For that reason, when Bob had suggested that the three of them hire Leif and Magnus to make a classic immigrant's trunk as a thank-you present, Jupiter had agreed to the plan.

But now he was thinking that the sheer amount of time it would take for the trunk to get made – and painted – might send the wrong signal, at least as far as Jupiter was concerned. The long labor behind the trunk might suggest that The Three Investigators were settling in for a long relationship with this girl, and although Jupiter was willing to admit that they *might* be, they also might not be. Only time would tell.

"Whichever way we make it, the trunk will be very beautiful," said Leif, showing both his sunny disposition and his optimism. "But I hope we can make a domed lid from red oak, which bends well."

"Sometimes," Magnus said gloomily.

Leif looked at his brother uncomprehendingly. "We've done this several times before. Remember the hatbox?"

"Yes," Magnus said. "I still have nightmares."

Jupiter smiled. "You heat the wood for the doming?" he asked Leif.

"Yes. With a steam box. First it must be cut very thin. We have some other projects we need to finish first, for your aunt's customers, but I'm sure we'll have the trunk ready in no time," Leif said.

"Let's not make any promises," Magnus said. "It may take us longer than you think."

Jupiter almost laughed this time. Leif and Magnus weren't twins, but they were two sides of a single optimism/pessimism coin. They were still talking about the trunk when Jupiter's Aunt Mathilda arrived. She was bubbling with excitement.

"There you are," she said to Leif and Magnus. "I just got off the phone with a woman who saw one of your dining room tables in a friend's house and wants one just like it."

She beamed, as pleased with herself for having hired them as she was with the brothers themselves.

"I've been going over Accounts Receivable and I can hardly believe how well we've been doing with your projects. I've decided to hire a website designer to reconstruct our website. I want to showcase your work; we'll take pictures of everything."

Leif and Magnus looked at her, surprised. Then a look of pleasure crept across Leif's face.

"I don't know," Magnus said. "Maybe it's too soon."

"Don't be silly, Magnus," Aunt Mathilda said. "You're always underestimating yourself."

His aunt's idea was a good one, Jupiter thought. Though the Salvage Yard had a website, it was extremely primitive – a single page with a picture of the entrance gates, the name of the enterprise, their address and the telephone number of the Salvage Yard's office, and a big banner headline that said "Come On In And Have A Look!!!!" That was it – hardly the sort of advertisement that generated any foot traffic, or even any interest. The website didn't even make it clear what "salvage" meant at present.

Jupiter was pleased for his aunt. She'd hired Leif and Magnus in the hopes that they would help the yard earn additional income. Apparently, it was working.

"I've also decided to hire someone who can help me take a complete inventory," Aunt Mathilda said. "I want to post a description and a picture of everything decent we have for sale here in the Salvage Yard. Lord knows, sometimes even I lose track of it all. And we could have a web store, so that people can make purchases online."

Jupiter nodded. Another excellent idea.

"I thought maybe I could hire this Mallory MacLeod," his aunt said, looking at him. "After all, she must like quality goods, or you boys wouldn't be having Leif and Magnus build her an immigrant's trunk. And since she's your age, I'm sure we can afford her!" She clapped her hands together and laughed heartily.

This annoyed Jupiter in more ways than one – but probably most because he didn't like the thought of his aunt taking advantage of Mallory. Which meant he must be starting to think of her as a friend. Which he really didn't want to. Not yet, at least.

"Oh, Jupiter, I didn't mean that," his aunt said, reading his mind. "Of course, we'd pay her the going rate. If she wanted the job, that is. Do you think she might want a job like that?"

"She might," Jupiter said reluctantly. "I

don't know for sure."

In fact, he *was* sure. He was sure she'd love it, and while everything he knew about Mallory made him think she'd also do an excellent job, he was quite nervous about how much his friends seemed to like her. Although he liked her too – or was beginning to – he certainly didn't want her showing up every time he and his friends were working on a case.

Still, he couldn't really say this to his aunt.

"Now what would be the best way to get in touch with her?" Aunt Mathilda asked. "Will you be seeing her anytime soon?"

"Not that I'm aware of," Jupiter said, quite truthfully.

"Do you have a phone number for her?" she asked.

When Jupiter nodded yes, Aunt Mathilda said, "Well, no time like the present."

Jupiter went to Headquarters – the hidden mobile home trailer where the boys gathered to discuss their cases – and returned with the number. As Jupiter emerged from Easy Three, Pete came sailing into the Salvage Yard on his bike.

"Hi, everyone," Pete said. "Jupe!"

Jupiter was joining his friend just as Bob

also arrived. Both Bob and Pete had gotten a little dressed up for their dinner with Isabella Chang.

"Hey, Jupiter!" Pete said. "Tell me the good news, you guys. Can we all go to Sonoma with my father this Sunday? He's got an intuition that something's really wrong!"

Jupiter had already asked his aunt and had gotten her permission.

"And I'm hoping he's right," he said. Jupiter liked and respected Mr. Crenshaw, and although there had been a time when Jupiter had thought "intuition" was just a word for not knowing anything for certain, lately he had started to think it might be more than that.

In fact, lately he had started to think that his own ability to draw connections between one thing and another might be rooted in intuition – that what was generally called deductive reasoning was really just a way of testing suppositions that arrived from the unconscious. If Mr. Crenshaw thought that something was going on on the set of *Bear Valley*, there was a good chance something really was.

"We need to find out more about this OUTLAW group, then," Jupiter said. "Whether they've engaged in sabotage before. The theft of that camera is serious. Even though OUT-

LAW can't really get on the set, they may have planted someone on the crew. Someone who's making life as hard as possible for everyone around him."

"Pete's father said they have a Facebook page," Bob said. "If it's public, I should be able to check them out."

"What does OUTLAW stand for, anyway?" Jupiter asked.

"Oh, we saw that on the news," Pete said. "It stands for "Outing Lawbreakers From Past Centuries."

"Outing Lawbreakers From Past Centuries," Jupiter repeated thoughtfully. "Was John Frémont a lawbreaker? All I know about him was that he was one of the first two Senators from California, and that he also ran for President in 1856 and lost."

"I think he actually became famous as an explorer and map maker," Bob said. "His reports about what he saw in the West had a big effect. People were really excited by his descriptions of the landscape, and they moved out west in droves. He didn't break any laws that I know of, but even if he did, the time to deal with that would have been when he was alive."

Pete added, "My father said that these days everyone is looking to pick a fight about something, and that these protesters seem to think that if California had stayed Mexican, the Indians would still own their land.”

“What happened to them was awful,” Jupiter said, “but this movie doesn’t seem to have anything to do with that. I wonder why this OUTLAW group picked it.”

However, before he could pursue this thought, his Aunt Mathilda approached them.

“Excuse me, boys,” Aunt Mathilda said. “I’m sure you’ve got important plans to make. But Jupiter, before it goes completely out of my mind, do you have that telephone number?”

Jupiter had scribbled Mallory MacLeod’s number on a piece of paper he had torn from a notepad, and in his excitement he had crumpled it a little. Abashed, he handed the paper to his aunt who made a great show of smoothing out the creases. She took her glasses off the top of her head where she had perched them. She peered at the paper. “The numbers are still legible,” she said.

“What’s that, Mrs. Jones?” Bob asked.

“It’s your friend’s telephone number,” Aunt Mathilda said. “Mallory MacLeod. I’m going to offer her a job working here in the Salvage Yard.”

Jupiter watched with some dismay as his

friends' faces transformed into masks of astonishment and pleasure as his aunt explained the job she was going to offer to Mallory.

"I think she'd be terrific," Bob said. "She knows an awful lot about old things."

"That's what I thought!" Aunt Mathilda said. "And we could use another woman around here." Her eyes moved from her husband to Leif and Magnus to the three boys.

"It's a great idea, Mrs. Jones," Pete said. "Didn't she say something about needing to get a job?"

"She definitely did," Bob said.

Leif and Magnus had roused themselves from the shade when Aunt Mathilda's piercing eyes had been directed at them. Now they walked over to join the group. They nodded hello to Pete and Bob.

"We've got those sketches ready," Leif said to Bob. "For the immigrant's trunk we're making. Why don't you come to the workshop and we can show them to you? We have two different sets of plans for you to choose from."

"I don't think they're ready to be looked at yet," Magnus grumbled. "We need to perfect them."

"Nonsense," Leif said. "We can always perfect them later. Now we need to find out what the boys' first impressions are."

Reluctantly, Magnus nodded agreement.

Jupiter smiled again. He liked the way the brothers balanced one another – how Leif's eagerness was kept in check by Magnus's natural reluctance, how Magnus's tendency toward naysaying was stabilized by Leif's natural enthusiasm.

"Gee," Bob said. "I'd love to see the sketches."

"Right this way," Leif said. He swept his arm in front of him as if inviting the boys to enter a grand room – though all he gestured toward was the Salvage Yard's gravel lot.

Jupiter followed the brothers and his friends. The interior of the brothers' workshop smelled of glue and freshly sawn wood. Jupiter loved it in there, but he rarely got the chance to visit.

Leif took the boys to a worktable where he unrolled a sheet of paper with carefully drawn sketches of the dome-lidded chest he and his brother proposed to build, with views of the side, the end, and the top, all drawn to scale and with the measurements of the final product clearly marked. The banding was beautifully proportional, and the top had just the right curve.

"That's really great-looking," Bob said cautiously, "and I'm sure it would show what you can do even better than a chest with a flat lid. But can I see the flat-lidded design, too? After all, you can sit on a flat-lidded trunk – or use it as a table – and you can't do that with a domed one. Also, I have the feeling that Mallory might be happier if we modeled ours on the one she liked in Grass Valley."

When Leif unrolled the other sketch, Jupiter could see at once that Bob was going to approve this design, rather than the one with the domed lid.

Bob nodded enthusiastically. "Mallory will love this," he said. "It looks exactly like the chest she admired in The Next Chapter Bookstore."

Jupiter and Pete agreed.

"It's super," Pete said. "But maybe you could make some other dome-lidded chests for customers of the Salvage Yard."

Magnus looked at Pete as though he'd lost his mind. "Let them ask for one first," he said.

The boys let Leif and Magnus return to work as they went back outside.

"What a day!" Pete said. "I haven't even told you about going to the Rescue Center yet!

And I can't wait to see Isabella Chang again."

"It was nice of her to invite us to dinner," Jupiter said. "You both look quite spiffy." He nodded approvingly. "Even though the case is closed, we still want to make a good impression. I have to shower and change. It'll take me about a half hour."

Pete looked at his watch. "She's expecting us at six-thirty. That should give us just enough time to get there."

"Can you keep busy while I'm gone?" Jupiter asked.

"I'd imagine so," Bob said.

"Well, don't do anything I'd do," Jupiter said, which made both of his friends laugh. He smiled and walked toward the gate at the back of the Salvage Yard which led to his aunt and uncle's house. He, too, was looking forward to seeing Isabella Chang again, but he was also excited about the possibility that there really *was* a mystery to solve on the set of *Bear Valley*.

Whether it was a simple one or a hard one, solving it would almost certainly be more gratifying than wrestling with the endlessly thorny question of why the human species could be so smart and so stupid at one and the same time.

As Pete's father had pointed out, nothing

could be stupider than venting a lot of outrage about people who had died long before you were born – especially because the only people you could punish were those who were alive right now. Unless you believed that the crimes of the parents should be visited on their children, there was just no logic to that at all.

Luckily, there were a lot of human beings who totally got that and who thought that any time they had left over from taking care of themselves and the people they were responsible for should be spent increasing the store of human knowledge and understanding.

That was certainly what Jupiter hoped to do with *his* life, he thought, as he sprinted up the stairs toward the shower, pulling his work shirt over his head.

3

On The OUTLAW Trail

After Jupiter vanished through the gate at the rear of the Salvage Yard, Bob sat on a lawn chair that Jupiter's aunt had placed invitingly near the office. He took his laptop out of his backpack and logged on to the office's Wi-Fi. He had time to do a bit of research about John Frémont and OUTLAW while he and Pete waited for Jupiter to get ready.

He'd liked doing the research on their last case, but writing up his report and posting it online had been even better. Bob thought it would help advertise their detective firm – especially because articles about Isabella Chang, the gold she'd inherited, and The Three Investigators had appeared in both the Rocky Beach *Herald* and the Los Angeles *Sun*.

But very few people had visited The Three Investigators new website yet. Bob had imagined that the Headquarters phone would ring off the hook with calls from people wanting to hire them, but they'd only gotten a few kook calls from people asking them to find more lost gold. Or imaginary lost gold.

Even so, Bob had loved writing the report. He'd been particularly proud of his idea to give all of their cases alphabetical titles from here on out. He'd called the first one *The Mystery of the Abecedarian Academy*, and the minute Pete's father had invited The Three Investigators to the set of *Bear Valley*, Bob had started wondering if he could use the word "bear" in his title, if this turned into a real case.

Still, since he was both Records *and* Research for The Three Investigators, that was only half his job. The other half – Research – was almost as good, and when he looked up Bear Valley, he discovered it was the name of a small town in the Sierra Nevadas, located on what had once been a ranch owned by John and Jessie Frémont. By a sort of accident, they'd bought a huge parcel of land just before gold was discovered in California and had become quite wealthy as a result.

While Bob was reading, Pete sat nearby, trying to be patient. Now he interrupted to ask what Bob was finding out about the movie.

"Not all that much yet. We already know it's based on the book *Bear Valley: A Prodigious Destiny*," Bob said.

"I even remember what prodigious means," said Pete. "Something that's really big.

Like a grizzly bear, compared to a black one, maybe."

"Or a Kodiac brown bear," Bob said. "I think they're the biggest bears there are."

"Could you believe when Mr. Munson told us they sometimes get orphaned black bear cubs to take care of?" Pete said. "I also thought it was interesting when he said we've always wanted to be the biggest and fiercest predators around."

"I don't know if that's what we've wanted, exactly," Bob responded. "I think it's more that we wanted to survive, and we killed other animals so they wouldn't kill us."

"Well, maybe. That bobcat didn't seem to exactly trust me."

Bob remembered that when he and Pete and Jupiter had been in Yosemite, talking about the animals who lived in the park, Pete had made a joke about the three of them having their own bobcat – a Bob-cat, he had said – and even though Bob had groaned at the joke, it had stuck with him. If he had had a spirit animal, maybe it would have been a bobcat.

"Have you found out anything about OUTLAW ?" Pete asked.

"Not yet," said Bob.

He rattled away on his keyboard and quickly found its Facebook page. As Bob and Pete studied OUTLAW's posts, they found that a man named Honon Miwok was playing an important role in organizing the protest against the movie. When they looked the name up, they discovered Honon meant "bear" in the Miwok language; his last name merely meant "the people."

"Bear!" said Pete. "That's pretty weird, don't you think?"

In his Facebook posts, Honon Miwok said he was a fully enrolled member of the Miwok tribe, and he argued quite forcefully that John Frémont was personally responsible for most of the attacks on Native Americans in California after the Bear Flag Revolt.

"This Honon Miwok is pretty convincing," Pete said. "He's trying to get people from San Francisco to travel up to Sonoma to protest the movie, and it looks like it's working. I can't believe the things the other OUTLAWs are saying. This guy named Dasan Coyote is really hot under the collar."

Bob and Pete were so engrossed in studying the pictures and the posts that they didn't even hear Jupiter coming back until he was standing right next to them.

Bob looked up, startled.

"You were certainly concentrating," Jupiter said.

"We were just reading about OUTLAW," Pete said. "They seem really set on messing with the filming of my dad's movie."

"I hope we can stop that from happening," said Jupiter. "Are we all ready?"

"I'm certainly ready to eat!" said Pete. He pulled from his pocket the antique pen nib he'd discovered on the site of the one-room schoolhouse at the center of their last case "We thought the museum in Auburn didn't need another one, so we decided to give it to Isabella Chang as a memento. Remember?" Pete said.

Bob was sure Jupiter *did* remember, since it had been his own idea.

However, all Jupe said was, "I certainly do. I'm sure she'll like that a lot. All right. Helmets on."

Just recently, Jupiter, Pete, and Bob had bought matching bike helmets. They'd gone shopping together – using firm funds – and now they each had a racing helmet in the color that matched the chalk they sometimes used to leave secret messages for one another.

Bob's helmet was green, while Pete's was blue and Jupiter's red. All three had fins as well as snappy gradings and striations, and as Pete strapped his on, Bob smiled as he remembered all the wild and wacky helmets Pete had had before this one. When he'd been ten he'd had a black and red Mohawk – the black bucket covered with triangular red patterns and the Mohawk part a bunch of rubber bristles sticking straight up and quivering – but when he was even younger, Pete had had a lime green helmet that looked like a cheerful shark.

Isabella Chang lived on a cul-de-sac in the southern part of town. It was a good-sized single-story house, made largely of redwood, with a gently sloping roof, a modern addition, and a front garden filled with carefully pruned shrubs. Even though Ms. Chang's eyesight was not what it had been once, she clearly could still see well enough to keep her place in tip-top shape, Bob thought.

The boys parked their bikes, took off their helmets, and straightened their clothes. Then Jupiter rang the doorbell. Bob was surprised when it was answered by a woman in her early thirties who they'd never seen before.

"The Three Investigators?" she said. "Come in!"

Bob searched for a word to describe the woman. "Odd" would do it, or "eccentric," but

Bob settled on "unconventional." She wore a colorful tie-dyed shirt and a wraparound many-colored skirt. A scarf of some flimsy material was draped around her neck. Her wrists were crowded with bangles, her fingers with rings. On her head was a tight red cap that resembled a turban. She looked a bit like a carnival fortuneteller, but she was warm and friendly and Bob decided that her clothing made her interesting and unusual. She introduced herself as Charlotte Mitchell and said she was Isabella Chang's part-time assistant.

"Now you must be Jupiter," she said, guessing correctly. "And Pete. And Bob."

"Wow!" Pete said. "How did you do that?"

"Isabella described you to me. She's very precise. Please come this way. She's in the living room."

She led the boys down a narrow hallway and past a closed door. On the walls on either side hung framed pages of very fancy writing — some of it Chinese characters and some of it English letters. The letters were carefully and beautifully shaped, identical in size and height. Though they formed intelligible words, the overall impression was of a piece of art rather than a piece of writing. Bob stopped short before one framed piece with characters on it that looked a lot like the ones on the eight Chinese talismans the boys had hung at the entrance to the Salvage Yard.

The living room was comfortably furnished and the wooden floors – mostly rugless – gleamed in the dim light. A low table held a number of African violets on a copper tray. Bob was struck by how orderly everything seemed, how peaceful the room was. Isabella Chang sat in an upholstered chair, an expectant expression on her face. When the boys entered the room, she broke into a smile.

"Welcome!" she said. "I'm so glad you could come to my house. "

As Charlotte left the room, the boys went over and shook Isabella Chang's hand. When it was Bob's turn, she took his hand in both of hers – which were warm and dry.

"Please call me Isabella," she said. "All of you. You did a beautiful job writing up the case for your website," she added to Bob. "Charlotte read it to me."

It turned out that Charlotte Mitchell helped Isabella out several times a week, doing the shopping and most of the cooking and driving her when she needed to go somewhere.

Jupiter and Bob murmured their thanks

as Charlotte came back, carrying a tray with five glasses filled with ice, milky at the bottom and darker at the top."

"I hope you like this," Isabella said. "It's lemonade and iced tea."

Bob took a sip. He found he did like it.

He cleared his throat. "There's a lot to talk about," he said, "but before we begin, could I ask you about the framed pictures in the hall?"

"Do you mean my calligraphy?" Isabella asked. "That was one of the many hobbies I had to give up when my eyesight got worse. Do you boys know about calligraphy?"

"Not much," Jupiter said. "Just that it's an ancient form of writing."

"And a modern one as well," Isabella said. "In China the art goes back over three thousand years. If you're really good, you can work with a brush or with a special pen, one with a nib."

Pete got to his feet, grinning. "Like this?" he asked. He walked over and put the pen nib he'd found in Isabella's hand.

"Charlotte," she said. "Would you bring me my magnifying glass?"

When she had gotten it, she stared down at the object in her hand. "Why, yes, Pete," she said. "Very like this. Where did this come from?"

"We found it at the one-room schoolhouse near Cool," Pete said. "The building was gone, but this was near the foundation. We wanted you to have it. As a souvenir."

"Why, thank you very much," Isabella said. "I'll treasure it. For all we know, my ancestor Li Chang might have used this – though frankly, I doubt it. As you know, those students were just learning their ABCs, and they did so by copying the samples their teacher gave them. The aim was to make perfect copies.

"In many ways that's what calligraphy is. Writing like that develops the delicate muscles in the hand and gives you great control. When I was doing calligraphy all the time, with a steel nib like this one, I did so much copying that I quickly got good at other people's handwriting." She laughed merrily. "Too bad I had no desire to be a forger! Are you boys hungry?"

Bob looked at Jupiter, who looked at Pete, who nodded his head firmly. Everyone chortled. "Well, let's go out back. Charlotte is going to cook a quick stir-fry. It shouldn't take long at all."

Isabella stood and Bob gallantly offered

her his arm, which she took with an amused smile. Together they led the way through a sliding glass door to the backyard. To Bob's amazement, it was big and open and welcoming − much bigger than his yard, or Pete's or Jupiter's.

Toward the back it had a wooden arbor completely covered with yellow roses. Mature trees, high bushes, and a lattice fence completely concealed the yard from the neighbors behind and to either side. It was a sort of secret garden − but a very large one, with a little pond.

Isabella saw Bob looking admiringly around him. "At the end of the school year, I always had my students here for a party. I miss those parties sometimes. Well, come sit next to the pond," she said.

They took their places around a round tiled table from which Bob could see golden fish swimming in the water.

"This, of course," Isabella Chang said, "is a koi pond. Those fish are a kind of carp. In ancient Asian culture, the pond symbolized love and friendship."

In no time, Charlotte had brought a tray with five plates on it. There was steamed rice and a chicken stir-fry with snow peas and thin strips of carrot. Charlotte pulled up a chair and they started to eat.

"So how did you boys meet Isabella?" Charlotte asked.

"Through our friend Hector Sebastian," Bob said.

"Ah, yes," Charlotte said. "Another writer."

"What do you mean?" Pete asked.

"Isabella's a writer, my aunt's a writer."

"Charlotte's aunt is having a movie made of her book," Isabella said. "I doubt they'll be making a movie about one-room schoolhouses any time soon."

"My aunt's book is about American history," Charlotte explained. "Her name is Phillipa Paxton."

All three of the boys looked at Charlotte incredulously.

"You mean the woman who wrote *Bear Valley*?" Bob said.

"Why, yes," Charlotte said. "Have you heard of it?"

"My dad built the sets for that movie," Pete said, "and the day after tomorrow, he's taking the three of us up to Sonoma to watch a day of filming."

"Well, you'll meet my aunt, then," Charlotte said. "They hired her as a consultant and she's already up there. At first it was all very exciting, but it hasn't turned out that well, I'm afraid."

"We heard there was some trouble," Jupiter said.

"She's had some very nasty things happen to her recently," Charlotte said. "Someone tore up the posters she had taped to her office door at the college where she teaches. Then, her tires were slashed. No one knows who's responsible, but it all started happening at about the same time this group began protesting the movie."

"You mean OUTLAW," Bob said.

Charlotte looked at him, surprised. "You boys seem to know everything," she exclaimed.

"We saw a news segment about the whole thing, and my father told us about it, too," Pete said.

"I've read Phillipa's book," Isabella said, "or Charlotte has read it to me. And as you know, I used to teach history. I must say, I'm extremely puzzled as to why anyone would be protesting either that book or a movie based on it. Of course, I'm sure very few, if any, of the protesters have read a word of it. They're all acting on hearsay. Phillipa's book is mostly about the marriage of John and Jessie Frémont, and there's certainly nothing in it that isn't true or accurate."

"I did some research on John Frémont," Bob said, "and he was pretty impressive. Those three expeditions into the west? He sounded not only like an explorer but also a scientist."

"That's exactly right," Isabella said. "But the real explorer was his guide, Kit Carson."

"Do you know a lot about him?" Pete asked. He sat up expectantly.

"I do," Isabella said. Bob could see how pleased she was to be talking to young people again – to have the chance to pass on her knowledge to them.

"He was a fur trapper and an Indian scout, a wilderness guide and a military hero," she said. "I did quite a bit of research on him when I was teaching. Of course my students were enthralled by him. He spoke I don't know how many languages – English, Spanish, and French, as well as any number of native languages, including Comanche, Apache, and Navajo. But he couldn't read or write."

"He couldn't?" Pete asked. "Why not?"

"Well," said Isabella, "his father died when he was nine and he needed to work to help support his family. He never got a formal education, and his life got so complicated that he just never learned. Other people wrote his letters for him – like Charlotte does for me, now – though he signed them himself."

"My grandparents never learned to read or write, either," Pete said.

"Many highly intelligent people have been illiterate," Isabella said. "Being able to read and write has really only been common in the last two hundred years. But Carson loved to be read aloud to. He was a funny man, small and bowlegged, unassuming and mild of manner. When strangers met him for the first time, they couldn't believe he was really the famous Kit Carson. They expected him to brandish pistols and drink heavily and swagger, but he wasn't like that at all.

"And he was filled with contradictions, like all of us. He was married three times, to an Arapahoe woman, a Cheyenne woman, and a Mexican woman. But he went to war against the Mexicans, and he waged war against the Navajo."

"Are you going to write a book about him?" Pete asked. "After you finish the one about Li Chang?"

Isabella Chang smiled. "That's a very

good idea, Pete. Maybe I will."

Charlotte brought dessert, and when the boys had finished their ice cream, Bob thought maybe it was time to go. Better not to overstay your welcome! He turned to Jupiter.

"I'm sorry," he said, "but there's some stuff I need to do at home."

Jupiter and Pete both got the hint and nodded.

"So soon?" Isabella said. "But then you must come again, before too long. We've hardly talked about Li Chang. I'm delighted with the way you've decided to divide up the money I want you to have. And when you buy your car and hire your driver, perhaps we could all go for a ride."

"That'll be a lot of fun!" Pete said.

They thanked Isabella again and again for her generosity – for the ten percent of the gold she was giving them, for the dinner and the conversation. It had been a good evening, Bob thought.

Isabella got to her feet. "Let me show you out," she said. "Charlotte, you come too."

As Isabella took them down the hallway lined with her calligraphy, she paused before the closed door they had passed earlier. "I should show you boys the wing," she said.

She opened the door and began walking down another hall.

"This is where my friend lived after she retired," Isabella said. "It's very nice and private. We often kept to ourselves, but in the evenings it was nice to have company."

She looked at the boys with a mischievous smile. "You did such a good job finding out about Li Chang, I thought you might find someone who wants a roommate. If you run into an older man in the course of your investigations who you think I'd like, please let me know. There's all this extra room, just going to waste."

"You bet!" Pete said, while Bob nodded. He thought it was great that Isabella was open to a new adventure, and to new friends. It was never too late.

"Now," Isabella said, "I'll say good night."

At the door, Charlotte shook their hands warmly.

"It was good to meet you guys," she said. "And I know how happy it made Isabella to see you. When you first walked in, she lit up like a chandelier."

"It was good to meet you, too!" Pete said. "Are you a fortune teller?"

Charlotte burst out laughing. "No," she said. "I just like to dress like one."

"Oh," Pete said. "Because I wondered if you knew my mother."

"Is she a fortune teller?" Charlotte asked.

"Not really," Pete said, flustered. "She's a fifth-grade teacher. But she believes in the Tarot and the I Ching and that sort of thing."

"I'd love to meet her," Charlotte said. "Now make sure you give my aunt my best when you see her up in Sonoma. And keep your eyes on those OUTLAWs."

"We will," Pete said. "Thanks!"

Bob followed Pete and Jupiter back to the Salvage Yard. It was cooler now, and the light was fading fast. They said good night and Pete took off in the direction of his house, while Bob headed toward his.

It had been a memorable evening, and even if they hadn't talked much about what had happened up in Auburn, it had been a great way to celebrate the successful conclusion of their earlier case. It might have been nice, Bob thought, if Mallory MacLeod had been there to celebrate with them. After all, she'd been quite instrumental in finding the gold.

Also, he liked her a lot and still couldn't

figure out why Jupiter kept holding her at arm's length. Well, he thought, the more Jupe sees her the more he'll like her. Perhaps she'd get the job at the Salvage Yard and then Jupe would see her all the time. That would be great, Bob thought. He certainly hoped it would happen. After all, Mallory's mother had promised she would take her back to Scotland if she couldn't get used to living in California during the next two years, and Bob already wanted her to stick around.

4

A Prodigious Opportunity

The following morning, Mallory MacLeod woke with a feeling of pleasant anticipation. The day before, Mathilda Jones had called to ask her if she'd like to apply for a summer job at the Jones Salvage Yard, and when she'd described the job, Mallory had said yes right away. She'd always liked making order out of chaos and she'd always loved old things, but even if she hadn't, she would have wanted to apply for a job at the Jones Salvage Yard. Ever since she'd ended up in Grass Valley at the same time that The Three Investigators were in Auburn, she'd been hoping to find a way to get to know them better.

Of course, in a way, she already knew them better than she would have if she hadn't been able to help them with the solution to their last mystery. In Auburn, the boys had thought they'd hit a dead end when they didn't know how to locate a pouch filled with gold without the map that marked its location. But there the map had been, in plain sight, and for reasons that had to do with the nature of her memory,

Mallory had discovered it.

She hadn't known that was what she was doing at the time, exactly, but in the end her powers of observation had proved crucial, and Jupiter Jones had invited her to be with The Three Investigators when they made their big discovery. She'd liked the way all of them had acted that day; Pete had been courageous, Jupiter smart, and Bob thoughtful.

And it wasn't just that she liked the boys as individuals; it was also that she liked what they – The Three Investigators – *did*. Ever since Mallory could remember, she'd been a voracious reader, and although she loved reading almost anything, she'd always found mysteries strangely soothing. She liked the way they were studded with clues, and she liked being able to read ahead to the ending to see where the writer was going, so she could notice the clues as she read along.

Although this meant that she rarely read mysteries as their writers intended, it had taught her a lot about what she now knew was called deductive reasoning. Something that at first appeared fantastic always proved to have a logical explanation in a mystery. Of course, in real life, the resolution of any riddle was unknown until you knew it, and Mallory had the feeling that the reason people liked mystery novels was that they made life seem more predictable than it actually was.

In real life, there were a lot of unexpected moments, and it therefore made sense that a lot of people would want to lose themselves in the logic of a mystery. The big puzzle called Life was reduced to a smaller puzzle – one that was solvable.

"Mallory?" her mother called from the living room. "Are you awake yet? I have to leave for work in fifteen minutes."

"I'm awake!" Mallory called back. She threw her legs over the side of the bed and hurried down the hall. She and her mother were currently living in an apartment in a Rocky Beach boarding house called The Wessex House, but as soon as their house in Scotland sold, they'd be buying a house of their own. After her father had died eight months before, Mallory's mother had decided to move the two of them back to Rocky Beach – where Mallory had actually been born.

When Mallory had protested as vigorously as she could – which was pretty vigorously – her mother had promised that if Mallory couldn't get used to life in America, they would move back to Scotland in two years. In the meantime, Mallory's mother hoped to work her way back to being a head costume designer – though the first job she'd gotten was more of a glorified seamstress on a movie filming locally. At the moment, she was designing and sewing a gigantic reproduction flag in a nearby warehouse rented by the production company.

"Sorry, Mom," Mallory said when she saw that her mother had set out a simple breakfast and made Mallory a cup of coffee. Mallory loved coffee, and every time she drank it, she thought of her father who had let her start drinking it when she was eleven.

"When are you due at the Salvage Yard for your interview?" Mrs. MacLeod asked.

"Not until 10:30," Mallory said. "I thought I'd return the books I took to Grass Valley on the way and get some new ones. I finally finished *Gulliver's Travels*. It was tough going by the end. But you know how much I hate to leave a book unfinished."

"So you got to the land ruled by intelligent horses?" her mother asked. "What did you think of the Yahoos?"

"I thought they were so vile I couldn't imagine why anyone would name an Internet search engine after them," Mallory said.

"I've wondered that myself," said Mrs.

MacLeod. "I have to hope we're better, in general, than the Yahoos. Though I have to admit that I've met a good many Yahoos in my life."

"Me, too," said Mallory. "Like my very own cousin, Skinny."

She had said this before, but was happy to say it again now.

"Oh, Mallory, he's not *that* bad," said her mother, smiling.

"Oh, yes, he is," said Mallory. "One of the reasons I'd like to get the job in the Salvage Yard is that Bob and Pete and Jupiter don't seem to hold it against me that I'm related to someone so Yahoo-like."

This time her mother laughed aloud. "Well, I've really got to go." she said. "Good luck with everything. I'll be back in time for dinner."

"Have a good day, Mom," Mallory said.

She ate breakfast, took a shower and got dressed, then packed her backpack with the books she was returning. After locking the door to the apartment, she got on her bike and started pedaling to the Rocky Beach Public Library. Although she'd known for almost two weeks now that in California kids under seventeen were supposed to wear bike helmets, she hadn't told her mother yet. She'd never used a bike helmet in her life, and though Bob Andrews had told her she could probably use her climbing helmet, she didn't want to.

For one thing, that helmet reminded her of her father, and for another, she liked the way the wind felt on her head when she was biking. Today was another beautiful summer day, and Mallory was already flushed from the heat. Since she'd lived in a cold and frequently cloudy climate nearly all her life, she was finding the endless blue skies and relentless sun of a southern California summer a bit hard to adjust to.

She wiped her hand across her forehead and it came away damp. She hadn't gotten more than a couple of blocks when she was struck again by the realization that Rocky Beach was a pretty small place; you constantly ran into people, even people you didn't want to run into.

Her cousin, Skinny Norris, was walking along the sidewalk whacking pebbles with a stick. One of them collided with the side of a parked car.

"Ouch!" Skinny said.

He was wearing plaid shorts and a black t-shirt with the name of some heavy metal band scrawled across it. When he noticed her, he called out gleefully, "Hey, Mally-Wally."

"How many times do I have to tell you not to call me that?" Mallory asked.

"O.K., Mally. Or Wally. Whichever you like," Skinny said. He guffawed and looked at her slyly. "So how are you? And how are your pals, The Three Little Investigators?"

She sighed and took a deep breath, trying to stay calm. "I don't know," she said. "I'll ask them the next time I see them." It surprised her how quickly Skinny could get to her.

Skinny's crewcut bristled and his Adam's apple bobbed. "Extually," he said, "I'm super glad I ran into you. Now I don't have to go to that smelly boarding house you're living in."

Since the boarding house *wasn't* smelly, the only effect this comment had on Mallory was to make her want to defend it from this undeserved attack.

"It's not smelly. I like it." Mallory stopped her bike and stood in the street, straddling it. "But why would you have to go there?" Mallory asked in a voice that sounded surprisingly like a growl to her.

Skinny grinned pathetically and sidled up to her.

"Sorry, Mally. Didn't mean to offend. My mom's planning a cookout by the swimming pool for Sunday afternoon. Hamburgers and barbecued ribs, that sort of thing. And she wanted to invite you and your mother."

"We're busy," Mallory said.

"Really?" Skinny said. "Doing what?"

"I don't know yet," Mallory said. "But we'll be busy."

"Ha ha ha," Skinny said. "About three in the afternoon, I think. Bathing suits optional." He grinned, a ghastly sight, and took off down the sidewalk whacking pebbles.

Mallory shook her head in disbelief, already planning to forget to tell her mother about the invitation. She jumped back on her bike and soon was fastening it to the rack outside the library. Inside, it was blessedly cool.

Mallory looked around, hoping to catch a glimpse of Bob Andrews. She put the books in the Circulation Desk's RETURNS slot and went off in search of further reading. After browsing for a while, she chose five novels and took them to check them out. She was quickly joined by Miss Bennett, the librarian.

"Well, hello," Miss Bennett said, smiling. "I hope you found something you liked last time."

"Yes," Mallory said. "I did, thank you. I was wondering. Is Bob Andrews here by any chance?"

"I'm afraid not," Miss Bennett said. "If you want, I can see when his next shift is scheduled."

"No, that's all right," Mallory said. "I'll see him next time, maybe." She put her new books in her backpack, slung it on, then took off for her interview with Mathilda Jones.

The day she'd first met Bob and Pete, she'd been bicycling past the Salvage Yard and had been brought up short by a fake suit of armor posed in a comic way she had thought was disrespectful.

Happily, the armor was gone now – though the eight Chinese talismans that had proved so important to The Three Investigators' last case still waved in the breeze. Mallory rolled through the gates and parked her bike, but when she found the office, no one was there.

She glanced at her watch and found she was fifteen minutes early, so she decided to look around the Salvage Yard to see what it had to offer. Some of the objects were stored in small buildings, some of them under roofs built like carports, and some of them were stacked along the inside of the fence around the yard. A pipe organ was prominently displayed, but also leaded glass windows, plumbing fixtures, ceramic tiles, interesting tools, fireplace mantels, old chandeliers, beautiful old doors and signs, and antique equipment and machines – as well as a lot of – well – junk.

Mallory opened the door of a workshop and startled two exceedingly tall and blond young men wearing safety goggles and working with hand sanders. When she introduced herself, the one who looked younger acted as though he'd just stuck his finger in a light socket, and the one who looked older said, smiling madly, "Why don't we talk outside?"

Once he had gotten her out of the workshop, he introduced himself as Leif and said Mallory should go back to the office and wait; he would call Mrs. Jones on the Salvage Yard intercom and tell her Mallory had arrived.

Mallory was walking back toward the office, wondering why the two men had hustled her out of their workshop as quickly as they had, when she encountered a man in his mid-fifties, wearing a pair of overalls and a bill cap.

Before she could say anything, he introduced himself. "I'm Titus Jones and this is my Salvage Yard. How can I be of service?"

Mallory shook his hand and told her why she was there.

"Ah, yes!" Titus Jones said. "Mathilda said you were interviewing today. Now, listen here, young lady. Depending on the day, my wife can be so distracted she won't know where she left her head, or so focused it can be downright frightening. Or something else entirely. Don't let her shake you. There's not a better woman on this planet, I promise you."

He looked toward the back fence where a gate had opened and closed, and a woman wearing a pair of jeans and a striped cotton shirt was fast approaching. She was stocky but she walked energetically, even forcefully.

"Ah, my dear," Titus Jones called. "I was just talking about you. Come hear this lovely Scottish accent."

Mallory watched with some alarm as Mathilda Jones charged her, her hand held out well in advance of any possible handshake. When the hands met, Mallory was almost knocked backwards.

"It seems she's focused today," Titus told Mallory. "For your information."

"Well," Mathilda Jones said. "I'm pleased to finally meet you. I've heard so much about you. Well, actually, that's not true, but I've certainly heard your name enough."

The woman stepped beside her, put her

arm around her, and started pulling her toward one of the sheds in the Salvage Yard. "Now, tell me all about yourself," she said.

Mallory thought that Mathilda Jones was a pretty strange woman, but all things considered, Mallory liked strange people. She told Mrs. Jones a little about Scotland and a little about her mother and as little about herself as she could get away with. If they got along, over time they'd get to know one another. There was no sense saying too much now.

Mrs. Jones flung open the door to a shed and flicked on the lights. This building was the size of a small barn; it had a loft on three sides and shelving up each of its walls. All the shelves were crammed with things, piled on top of each other. There were a lot of things.

A lot.

"So how did you get interested in old things?" Mathilda Jones asked.

"I don't really know," Mallory told her. "The house we first lived in when we moved to Scotland, when I was still a baby – well, we rented it for several years and it was crammed with antiques and things that had been in the family for generations. Those were some of the earliest things I played with. I mean, I didn't

79

really play with them, but I looked at them and – well, I got to know them. Later, I learned that I liked almost all material culture. Not cars, but buildings, clothing, art and artifacts, and tools.”

“I know exactly what you mean,” Mrs. Jones said. “Now, as you can see, we’re a bit disorganized. I was hoping to find someone who could create some kind of order, could sort like with like, and valuable from not-so-valuable. To put it plainly, some of this is just junk and we should be looking to get rid of it. But there’s plenty of wonderful stuff, too, and I think you might have just the eye to sort out the pearls from the swine, if you know what I mean. The wheat from the chaff. Do you think you could do that?”

Mallory looked at her and nodded. “Yes,” she said. “I have an eye for the authentic, and authenticity generally translates into value.”

Mrs. Jones thumped Mallory on the back. “My Lord! A fellow traveler!”

“So I’ll do some sorting, and then you can take a look – ”

“Oh, no,” Mrs. Jones said. “If I hire you – and I have every intention of hiring you – you’ll be on your own. I trust young people to make the right decisions if you give them real responsibility. I've always trusted Jupiter and he hasn't let me down yet. And since you're a friend of his and a friend of his friends, I thought you'd be the someone I was looking for. Someone who doesn't need supervision. Someone who can work on her own, who's self-directed, and who likes old things."

Mallory nodded. That actually sounded pretty great.

"Now I also want you to take pictures. We have a camera you can use, and we'll upload the pictures to the new website I'm having designed. You'll sort everything and organize everything and inventory everything. You'll need to put stickers with bar codes on the backs of most of the objects, and keep track of what is what. The person designing the website will provide you with the stickers, with their barcodes, but you'll need to keep track of them."

Mrs. Jones was speaking so rapidly that Mallory could barely catch her breath. All the while, the woman was escorting her from one end of the shed to the other, picking up objects and putting them down, and all without pausing in her non-stop description of the work to be done. It seemed like a wonderful job, Mallory thought, even if Mrs. Jones was making her dizzy.

At last Mrs. Jones seemed to run out of steam. Her cheeks were bright red and her eyes seemed focused on a future of perfect order, in which everything was sorted and photographed and inventoried and catalogued.

"Now take a look at these," she said.

She dragged Mallory to a corner of the shed where a large number of old signs had already been sorted. Some were hand-painted on wood, others screen-printed on galvanized steel. Some were obviously one-of-a-kind, while others were replicas and reproductions. They had been stacked against one another.

Mallory looked through them, amazed at their variety. One hand-painted sign advertised a boatyard in San Diego and seemed to date from the late 19th century. In the middle was a schooner with two masts, all its sails aloft, on a calm sea. Another was from a dude ranch in the Sierra and had the outline of a cowboy on a bucking horse and the name: *Hell Dorado*. A third was stamped metal and hand-painted, selling Murphy Motor Car enamel. On it, a man with slicked-back hair and a blank expression was painting the hood of an old motorcar the shocking red of nail polish.

Each one of the signs interested Mallory.

They all had stories behind them; someone had thought about how best to communicate to other people – to advertise or sell or simply signify – and then had gone to the trouble to design it and create it. Each sign was interesting but with the story in Mallory's head, it became almost like a novel.

"I don't know what you think, Mrs. Jones," she said, "but along with the photograph and the description, it might be a good idea to include a sort of story about each item so that people could feel – I don't know – something personal about it."

"Why, Mallory," Mrs. Jones said. "That's an absolutely terrific idea. Could you give me an example?"

Mallory poked through a few more of the signs until she came to a Coca-Cola sign – red script on sheet metal, the old-fashioned logo. She held it up so Mrs. Jones could get a good look. "Like this one," she said. "It looks like it hung outside a country store, letting people know that Coke was for sale. So, something like: *Remember that Coca-Cola you had on that summer day when you were a kid, the way you walked into that store out of the blazing sun, and the old man handed you an ice-cold bottle?* I don't know. Something like that," Mallory finished.

Mrs. Jones looked at her, astonished. "Why, child," she said. "Did you just make that up? Right then? That was wonderful! Who could resist buying that sign with that little story attached? You're hired! You can start right away, with these signs, if you have the time. Just a few hours today, but then as often as you can get here and want to earn some money. Make your own schedule. You can see how much work there is to do."

Mrs. Jones gave her a big smile and then a sideways hug. Older women were always doing that, and Mallory didn't understand whether it was to try to make her feel better or to make themselves feel better. Any which way, she felt good, she felt fine, she felt terrific. She felt hired!

Mrs. Jones left the shed, and Mallory followed her. She thought she might as well take a look around the rest of the Salvage Yard to see what else needed sorting and describing. She was peering under a tarpaulin at a pile of what looked to be large architectural moldings when she heard the sound of tires on gravel and looked up to see Pete Crenshaw ride up on his bike.

The last time they'd been together had been about a week before, in an old Carnegie

Library in Auburn, California – where Pete had tackled a grown man who was trying to steal a sack of gold nuggets while she had pushed a wheeled chair into the legs of his accomplice. She felt this had given them a bond and smiled with genuine pleasure.

Pete waved to her as he dismounted and took off his helmet. He looked cute in it, really, she thought. Well, not cute, exactly, but not *not*-cute either. If she had to get a bike helmet, maybe she could get one like his.

"Hey, Mallory!" Pete called out. "Jupe's aunt said she was going to offer you a job. Did you get it? Are you starting already?"

"Yes," Mallory said. "Mrs. Jones showed me around and I guess I impressed her. She said I could start today and keep my own hours."

"That's fantastic!" Pete exclaimed. "I've got a new job, too! Except I don't get paid for mine. I'm volunteering at the Rocky Beach Animal Rescue Center. I saw a wild red fox with hair almost as red as yours."

Although Mallory knew this was intended as a compliment, she just said, "I've always liked red foxes. There are a lot of them in Scotland. They eat mice and voles."

"What are voles?" Pete asked.

"Small rodents," Mallory said. "A lot like mice, but their ears are smaller. I don't think Jupiter's here," she added. "At least I haven't seen him."

"I didn't come to see Jupe," Pete told her. "I left some stuff here I need to pack. My dad's taking the three of us up to the set of the movie he's working on in Sonoma. It's called *Bear Valley*. He said there might be some trouble and he wants us to keep our eyes open."

"Trouble? What kind?" Mallory asked, with real concern. *Bear Valley* was the movie her mother was working on right now − although she wasn't in Sonoma, but in a warehouse not far from Rocky Beach. If there was trouble about the movie, it might spread.

"Things being stolen and, damaged," Pete said. "Also, a protest group called OUT-LAW. They have a Facebook page, and they've organized a campaign to try to shut the movie down."

"Good grief," said Mallory. "I hope my mother doesn't lose her job. She really needs it. *We* really need it. These online vigilante groups are like the Yahoos in a book I just read."

"Your mother's working on the movie, too?" Pete exclaimed in astonishment.

"Right now she's working in a warehouse not far from here. She's usually a costume designer, but on this movie she's really just a seamstress, and she's making a replica of a flag."

Pete looked very interested. "The Bear Flag?" he asked.

"She already made that," Mallory said. "The one she's working on now is a replica of a flag John Frémont's wife had made for him as a present. It's 15 feet by 20, my mother told me. That's why she's making it in a warehouse."

"15 x 20!" said Pete. "That's prodigious!"

Mallory smiled. "You could almost say it's Brobdingnagian."

"Brob what?" Pete asked. "That sounds made up."

"It *is* made up," said Mallory. " It's from that book I told you about, the one with the Yahoos. *Gulliver's Travels*. Gulliver goes to another country called Brobdingnag, which has a race of giants, and where everything is huge."

"Brob-ding-nagian," Pete repeated carefully. "I'll have to remember that. Who exactly are the Yahoos?"

Mallory explained to him as best she could. "They're coarse and brutish and too much like a lot of human beings for my taste." She went on until she looked up to see Jupiter approaching. He nodded hello to both of them and then stood a little awkwardly to the side.

"Hey, Jupe," Pete said, "where have you been?"

"I was in the house deciding what to take to Sonoma."

"Well, remember," Pete said, "it's only for two days. Guess what? Mallory's mother is also working on *Bear Valley* – though she isn't going to be on the Sonoma set."

Jupiter said, "I'm sorry to hear that," but Mallory could see that, if anything, he was relieved to learn that her mother wouldn't be there when The Three Investigators got to Sonoma. She was glad that Bob and Pete so obviously liked her, because Jupiter would clearly be a harder nut to crack.

"Have fun up there," she said. "Your aunt gave me the job, so I'm sure I'll see you when you get back."

She said goodbye to the boys, then went to the office to sign in on a time sheet so that she could start her new job right away. Even though it wouldn't pay much, it was what you might call a prodigious opportunity to establish a new life for herself in Rocky Beach.

Of course, even now, she wasn't sure she wanted to do that, but since she knew that she would need to stay in America for two entire years before her mother would agree to take her back to Scotland, it would be good to have something interesting to do in the meanwhile.

Also, if she hung out long enough at the Salvage Yard, maybe she'd have the chance to help The Three Investigators solve another mystery. Though it had been sweet when Pete had talked about the color of the wild red fox's hair at the Animal Rescue Center, she hoped that he and Bob and Jupiter would all be willing to see past the way she looked to the way she actually *was*.

5

Dueling Historians

The next morning, Pete was up before daybreak, eager to get going, and after he and his father picked up Bob and his bike, they were off to the Salvage Yard where Jupiter was waiting. Pete's father made sure all three bikes were secured in the back of the shiny red pickup, and then they were on their way – Pete in the front with his father, and Jupiter and Bob in the back seat of the cab.

Although they were very different, Pete not only loved his father, he really respected him, and was sometimes almost awed by the way he handled the details of his life. Martín Crenshaw came from a large Mexican-American family – his parents had had four children and now all of them were married and had children of their own – so Pete was awash in aunts and uncles and cousins, the youngest of whom he sometimes baby-sat.

Ever since Pete could remember, his father had impressed on him the importance of family, and beyond that, of the greater community in which he lived. Over the years Pete's father had gotten involved in local issues he thought important – like the time the school board had threatened to stop funding vocational classes at the high school, and he and Bob's father had worked together and had managed to save them.

Now, as they headed for Sonoma, Pete was not only feeling pumped that his father had asked The Three Investigators to come with him to the set of *Bear Valley*, he was also feeling determined to prove himself by figuring out what was going on there, particularly when it came to the matter of Daniel Hernández!

It was a straight shot up Interstate 5 – all the way through the Central Valley – and sitting next to his father, Pete was able to talk with him for much of the drive. Pete's mother's sister Lilliana lived with her Anglo husband, David Robertson, on a small citrus ranch not far outside of Bakersfield, and as they passed the road they'd have turned off on if they'd been going to visit the Robertsons, Pete's father remarked on how everyone on the set of the movie in Sonoma was eating Central Valley oranges as if they weren't making them any more.

"The woman who wrote the book the movie is based on can't seem to get enough," he said, laughing. "I like her. She's very *real*. She grew up in Wyoming – where there's a mountain named after John Frémont. She may be a historian and a college professor but she dresses like a cowgirl – and probably rides like one, too!"

"Wyoming!" Pete exclaimed. "I can't believe I forgot to tell you," he added. "Hector Sebastian is moving to Wyoming!"

"He is?" Pete's father asked. "Why in the world?"

"He wants to go back to writing old-fashioned mysteries and he thinks Wyoming will inspire him. The last time we saw him, I told him about that time you almost worked on that movie ranch there, and he knew all about it," Pete said. "I can't remember what it's called."

Martín Crenshaw turned and stared at him. "The Malachi Wagner Movie Ranch. It's funny you should mention it. I just read in a trade magazine about a film in development about the son of the man the ranch is named after. It seems that he was a dinosaur nut and moved to Wyoming to hunt dinosaur fossils."

"I didn't know there were dinosaurs in Wyoming!" Pete said. "Do you remember when we saw *Jurassic Park*?"

"Of course," said his father. "I remember all the movies we've seen together." He started counting them on the steering wheel. "*Jurassic Park* and *The Terminator* and *The Fifth Element* and *The Deer Hunter* and – well, all of them, I think!"

Pete remembered all of them, too. One thing he and his father totally had in common was loving movies. Which reminded him of another thing –

"And I also forgot to tell you that when we were up in the Gold Country, Worthington told us that one of his grandfathers was from India. A Lascar who settled in England!"

Even though "Lascar" wasn't the most common word in the world, Pete knew that his father would know what it meant. A year or two before, Martín Crenshaw had worked on a movie about the 18th-century British Navy. The star had been a famous Indian actor named Raj Khan, and Daman Duwalia, one of Pete's favorite young actors who he knew from the *Time Twist* series, had had a small role in it.

Pete had learned while watching the movie that Lascars had been Indian sailors employed on European sailing ships. He'd also had a lot of fun with his father. Which he was planning to have again – if they ever got to

Sonoma. It seemed to be farther from Rocky Beach than Pete remembered.

South of the Bay Area, Mr. Crenshaw turned west, then north, and by early afternoon they'd finally arrived. They hadn't stopped during the ride and although they *had* brought a few snacks with them, Pete was starving.

"Just hold out a while longer," his father told him. "The buffet lunch I told you about is worth waiting for."

At last, Mr. Crenshaw parked the truck, and all four of them clambered out. The producers of *Bear Valley* had secured permission to shoot at the original barracks where the Bear Flag Revolt had occurred – now in Sonoma State Historic Park, which bordered the central downtown Sonoma Plaza. The barracks was a two-story adobe building with a wide second-story balcony and a red tile roof.

As Pete looked around, he could see the still-visible remnants of the past – several storefronts retained their old adobe façades, and the alleyways were narrow and crooked — but most of the buildings surrounding the plaza seemed distinctly 21st-century commercial enterprises.

Pete was really proud of his father as he pointed out how his crew had removed all traces of the present day from the area they'd be using in the film — gone were the traffic signs and signals, the streetlights and utility poles and wires, the concrete planters with petunias. The asphalt street had been covered with red dirt and straw, and the crew had otherwise disguised and distressed the adjacent buildings so they looked as they had in 1846.

Because the barracks was now a museum, they would only be able to use the exterior; Pete's father had built a replica of the interior, as it had been at the time of the revolt, on a lot not far away. But here, on the edge of the plaza, the illusion was complete.

As it turned out, the plaza's center was an eight-acre park. The entire area near the barracks and the old Spanish mission had been cordoned off, and Pete could see throngs of tourists craning their necks to get a view of the action. Only there was no action at the moment. The plaza baked in the afternoon sun, and the barracks – where the actual Bear Flag had been raised – looked abandoned.

"Boys," Pete's father said. "I've got to check in with Richard Black. You can take care of yourselves for a while, right?"

Pete and the others assured him that they could.

Pete's father checked his watch. "I'll meet you over there – " He pointed beyond the set to a place where long tables and chairs stood empty. " – in about forty minutes or so. Hope you'll all be hungry by then."

"Forty minutes?" Pete groaned.

"You'll live," his father said. "I promise."

As Mr. Crenshaw walked away, Pete looked around, a bit dazed, wondering what they'd do before it was time for serious eats. But even before he could confer with Jupiter and Bob, he saw a man he recognized heading right toward them. He looked at Bob, whose expression had frozen, staring in the man's direction.

Daniel Hernández wore expensive-looking sunglasses, pleated trousers, and a light blue crinkly shirt, and he walked with the loose-limbed gait of a natural athlete. Around his neck was a lanyard with a laminated ID card. To Pete he looked about the same age as his father.

"Are you Pete Crenshaw?" Hernández asked, taking off his sunglasses. "I just saw you talking to Martín, and the other day he told me his son might be visiting the set. You look just like him."

The man had arching eyebrows and very

dark eyes, and he was smiling warmly, as if he had known Pete all his life. Pete took a step backward, so forceful was the man's approach.

Hernández turned to Jupiter and Bob. "And if he's Pete, then you two must be the rest of The Three Investigators." Pete's heart sank. They were supposed to be here undercover! And here they were, outed during the first half hour.

"How do you know about The Three Investigators?" he asked.

"You're practically celebrities," Daniel Hernández said. "After your escapade up in Auburn, there were all sorts of articles about you in the L.A. and San Francisco papers. I looked you up online and read all about you. Not everyone discovers gold hidden for over a hundred years."

Jupiter smiled thinly.

"We haven't been introduced," he said coolly. "I'm Jupiter Jones."

"A thousand pardons," the man said. "I'm Daniel Hernández. I've been hired – "

"Yes," Jupiter said. "We know."

"Bob and I saw you on TV," Pete said, trying to keep his voice as neutral as possible. "You're sort of a celebrity, too."

"I wouldn't say that," Hernández cooed,

but Pete could tell that he liked the idea.

"My father told me all about you," he said meaningfully.

"Did he?" Hernández said, an edge of steel suddenly appearing in his honeyed voice. "What a wizard your father is." He turned his attention fully to Pete. "Look at the work he and his crew have done!" He swept his arm in the direction of the barracks. "Most days this is a bustling 21st-century town center, but Martín has aged it a hundred and seventy years."

Pete remembered his father saying he would have liked to punch Daniel Hernández's lights out and he was beginning to understand why. Though the man was working overtime at being friendly, Pete felt it was all an act, and it grated on him.

"What are you boys working on now?" Daniel Hernández asked.

"We're between cases, actually," Jupiter said. "We're just visiting."

"Well, it's great to have young people on the set," Hernández said. "I'm sure you'll enjoy seeing the start of the Bear Flag Revolt. There's nothing like a recreation to make you excited about history."

"Mr. Crenshaw said you wrote a book about John Frémont," Jupiter said.

"Why, yes, I did," Daniel Hernández said. "That's the reason I was hired to consult on this film. Would you boys like me to show you around? Perhaps we could visit the museum together."

Though that sounded less than enjoyable to Pete, he thought it would give him more of a chance to observe Hernández, and besides, the buffet would still not be open for half an hour.

"A historian taking us on a guided tour of a history museum," Jupiter said. "What could be better?"

Bob was trying to suppress a smile.

Just inside the door of the museum, Pete saw a cannon with big wheels and a short black barrel. "How old is that?" he asked Hernández.

"It dates from the mid-1800s," Hernández said, "but it's very well-preserved." He pointed out the curved metal bands securing the wooden wheel rims. "Beautiful work," he said.

Hernández led the boys further inside. There was a display with a replica of the Bear Flag – the original of which, Hernández said, had been made in this very building.

One whole room was dedicated to showing how the soldiers lived – whitewashed walls, a dark wood-beamed ceiling, low wooden beds with storage trunks at their feet, the table where they ate and played cards. Everything was colorful and vibrant, as though it had all happened yesterday. Although Pete wasn't a history buff the way that Bob – and even Jupiter – were, in a museum like this one he couldn't help but think about what it must have been like to be one of the original American settlers of this area when there were twenty-five Mexicans for every American – and who knew how many Indians?

"You're very kind to let me share my passion for history with you," Hernández said. "During the summer I miss having the opportunity to talk with young people. I find them so much more open and responsive than most adults." Pete had to restrain himself from rolling his eyes. The guy was laying it on with a trowel.

"I heard some colleges are cutting history departments," Jupiter said.

"Unfortunately, true," Hernández said. "Everyone's nervous about enrollments, and our culture, I'm afraid, is terribly shortsighted. But our department is thriving. In fact, one of the things I like most about my job is advising prospective majors, because I get to answer the great question: Why History?"

He paused for dramatic effect. "Because it's the story of all of us, of course. How can we know where we're going without a thorough knowledge of where we have been?"

Oh, put a sock in it, Pete thought.

"Any of you considering a major in History?" Hernández asked. "You look like the sort of young men who think ahead."

"We haven't gotten that far," Pete said. "We're just starting high school in the fall."

"Nevertheless," Hernández said, "the child is father to the man. An interest in history can begin quite early. If you'd ever like to talk about it, I hope you'll give me a call."

He pulled out a small silver case from the front pocket of his pants and took out a card, which he presented to Jupiter. Pete looked over Jupiter's shoulder. Though the card had the appearance of being hand-lettered, Pete could see that it had been printed. Dr. Daniel Hernández, and the address at the university in Los Angeles where he taught, had been written in careful calligraphic script and gave the immediate impression of old-fashioned elegance and formality.

"That doesn't look like a font," Bob said.

"No," Hernández said. "It's not. That's my own handwriting. Well, it's a facsimile of my own handwriting." Below his address was the name of his book. *Manifest Murder: John Frémont and the Taking of the American West*. It seemed calculated to cause a commotion, Pete thought, even just sitting on the page like that.

"I was silly not to bring any copies with me, but when I'm back down in L.A., I'd be delighted to send The Three Investigators a signed copy. Where should I send it?"

Pete looked at Jupiter. Normally this was when Jupiter would reach into his pocket and produce one of The Three Investigators' business cards with a flourish. But it was clear that wasn't going to happen today.

"You said you found us online," Jupiter said. "Our address is on the website."

"Of course," Hernández said. "It was very impressive. I'll keep you boys well in mind if there's a mystery that needs solving." His eyes glinted.

When they emerged into the afternoon sunlight, Pete was dazzled by the brightness. In the distance he heard what sounded like people yelling. "It seems that OUTLAW has arrived," Hernández said. "More of them every day. I was afraid that might happen."

"I thought the movie hired you to make them happy," Bob said. "Why are they still here?"

"They have a point to make," Hernández said, "and I guess they're intent on making it, whether or not I'm involved in the movie. That's one of the things that makes this country great, of course. Freedom of speech." He looked at the boys and nodded his head. "Well, I must be off. It was a pleasure to meet the three of you," he said. "I really hope we run into each other again."

"I'm sure we will," Jupiter said. He was holding himself very still and looking at Hernández with icy regard.

Hernández held out his hand, and Pete didn't know how he couldn't take it. When they shook, he was surprised that Hernández's grip was almost as strong as Pete's father's.

His voice caught in his throat but he managed to croak out, "Nice meeting you, Dr. Hernández."

"Let's not have any of this 'doctor' stuff," Hernández said. "Now that we're friends, I insist you call me Daniel."

"Gee," Pete said. "We usually address adults formally."

"Well, this is where you learn to break

the habit," Hernández said.

"I don't think so," Jupiter said. "We appreciate the courtesy but we'll need to wait for some other time to take advantage of it, Dr. Hernández."

Hernández looked taken aback. He put up his hands in a gesture of surrender. "Far be it from me to say otherwise," he said. "I hope you enjoy your visit." He gave a short informal bow, turned on his heel, and was soon gone from view.

"A complete and thorough jackass," Bob said. "He's worse in person than he was on television."

"Yes," Jupiter said. "Unfortunate. He's a slippery one. We're going to need to keep an eye on him."

You bet, Pete thought. That's just what I intend to do.

Pete's stomach was now growling, but Jupiter said, "I'd like to get a closer look at this OUTLAW group." He led the way into the plaza. As they approached the sawhorse barricades and the sagging lengths of yellow KEEP OUT tape, the voices grew louder, reaching a shout. A few policemen stood well back, their feet shoulder-width apart, their hands clasped behind their backs.

On the other side of the sawhorses, pressed against them, was a crowd of men and women, many of them young. They wore black t-shirts and black bandanas and carried picket signs. Some just held pieces of poster board emblazoned with slogans, one of which read "U.S. Out Of North America!" They were chanting in unison, punctuating their shouts with raised fists. "No John Frémont! No naiveté! No more living in an invader's USA!" they yelled.

Although Pete was no expert on protests or group chants, he found OUTLAW's chant peculiar. *Naiveté* was a strange rhyme for *USA*, it seemed to him.

Suddenly, as Pete and Bob and Jupiter watched, a young man who was standing about ten feet behind the sawhorses surged forward, pushing people aside. The noise grew, as other protesters tried to stop him, but by then he was just the vanguard of a group determined to break through the barricade. His eyes looked wild, and if he had had talons, he would have had them out, Pete thought. Instinctively, he stepped back. He remembered the way the great horned owl's talons had pierced the leather gloves – though, unlike the owl, this man would have hurt Pete on purpose if he could have.

In fact, he started shouting, directly at The Three Investigators. "Get out of my valley! Get out of California! I wear the skin of the grizzly bear!"

There was now general shouting and shoving. One of the sawhorses was knocked over and the tape broke, its ends fluttering in the wind. Pete found himself remembering what Mallory MacLeod had told him about Yahoos. These people seemed worse than that, really. And they were real, not fictions in a book.

Some policemen quickly moved in, their truncheons ready. At the sight of them approaching, the crowd drew back. Soon enough, order — or so it seemed — had been restored. The man who had been shouting was pulled back by those around him, and the police once again stood impassively on one side of the sawhorses, with the protesters on the other. The chant resumed.

Pete was alarmed at how quickly everything had changed – how suddenly people had gotten angry, and how easily the peaceful protest could have turned into a violent one. It was as though people stopped being themselves and became part of some enormous, mindless creature when they were in a large group.

He'd had enough of OUTLAW. "Let's get out of here," he said to Bob and Jupe, and they quickly agreed.

While the boys had been in the museum, the catering company had set up the buffet, and the tables were now loaded with platters and baskets and steam trays. Pete loved buffets – so many different foods and so much of them.

He caught sight of his father, already in line, and he waved frantically. "Come on," he said urgently to Bob and Jupe and hurried to join his father.

"I didn't know where you three had gotten to," Mr. Crenshaw said. "I thought perhaps you'd lost your appetites."

"That's a good one," said Pete. "We ran into Dr. Hernández – or rather he ran into us – and he showed us through the museum."

"You don't say," Mr. Crenshaw said, an inscrutable expression on his face.

From where Pete stood in line, he thought he could see a big bowl of fruit salad, but everything else was a mystery. Boy, was he hungry! A bit ahead of them in line stood a tall older woman wearing cowboy boots, Levis, and a checked shirt with pearl snap buttons. She had a canvas messenger bag slung over one shoulder, and her face was shaded by a cowboy hat. Pete thought she must be Dr. Paxton. While the four of them loaded up their plates — and with lots better food than fruit salad — his father confirmed that he was right. He introduced them to the historian, and soon they were all sitting together at a table.

"So you're from Wyoming?" Pete asked. "And we just met your niece, Charlotte, at Isabella Chang's house!"

"You met Charlotte?" she asked. "How nice!"

Soon, he was telling her about how "a friend of theirs" had moved to Wyoming, and she was telling them that there was a Frémont County in Wyoming, and a Frémont Lake, near Pinedale. Frémont Peak, which had first been climbed by John Frémont and Kit Carson, was the third highest peak in the Wind River Mountains.

"Where is your friend living?" she asked Bob.

"In a town called Dubois," Bob said. "Actually, on a ranch outside of it somewhere. His name is Hector Sebastian, and he's a mystery writer we met on one of our first cases."

"Hector Sebastian!" said Dr. Paxton.

"I'm impressed. I've read a couple of his mysteries. And, by the way, Dubois is also in Frémont County! I don't think there's a state in America which doesn't have *something* named after Frémont."

She looked irritated for a moment. "There's no question that the indigenous populations of the Americas lost their lands after the European conquest, but there's no reason on earth to blame John Frémont," she said. "Not only did he and his wife Jessie play a very important role in making sure that California entered the United States as a free state, not a slave one, but at heart he was a scientist – and also something of a poet.

"He named the Golden Gate Strait, the Great Basin, and Pyramid Lake in Nevada, and identified and named any number of North American flowers. Most amazing of all, even though he wasn't a hydrographer, he figured out that none of the water in the Great Basin flowed into the sea! He was really a kind of investigator – just like the three of you. And that reminds me. I don't know if you boys are working on a case right now, but I have a mystery I could use some help solving," Dr. Paxton said.

"Really?" Pete said. He wondered if maybe she was going to ask The Three Investigators to look into the strange events her niece had told them about at Isabella Chang's, but when she went on, it was about something else entirely.

She explained that she and her husband collected memorabilia connected to John and Jessie Frémont, and that she'd been trying to track down a specific item for some time now. It was a large flag based on the Bear Flag which Jessie Frémont had had made for her husband as a birthday present.

"Wow!" Pete said. "I think that Mrs. MacLeod is making a copy of that flag for the movie. Mallory told me it was gigantic − 15 x 20, I think she said. And you're looking to find the original?"

"Mrs. MacLeod's daughter Mallory is a friend of ours," Bob explained.

"I've met her mother, but not her," Dr. Paxton said. "Unfortunately, the original was lost in the fires that raged after the 1906 San Francisco earthquake. But since the seamstress Jessie hired became quite famous, someone who was collecting her work had a replica of the original made."

"What's the mystery regarding it?" asked Jupiter with real interest.

"Well, as I said, it's not *really* a mystery,

but I've found multiple conflicting reports of something called 'Jessie and John Frémont Commemorative Bear State Flag, with flowers and mountain scene' being sold privately all the way up to the mid-1990s. The last mention was in the Sonoma *Record* in 1998," Dr. Paxton said. "There was a picture of the house belonging to the man who owned it. Then the trail goes cold."

Pete had a bit of trouble following Dr. Paxton's explanation but it seemed that the article had been about Sonoma houses that contained art collections of some kind – though, for reasons of privacy, the reporter had omitted the addresses and owner's names. All Dr. Paxton had was a copy of the newspaper photograph of the house the man had lived in back in 1998, along with a photo of the quilt he'd owned.

She pulled Xerox copies of two grainy black and white photos from her messenger bag.

"The house is an Arts and Crafts house," Dr. Paxton said. "Although a lot of Arts and Crafts houses were built from kits, this one has an unusual central chimney, and I half-expected I'd just stumble across it driving around town. I've also shown the photo to several people. But so far, no luck.

"I don't know if you're interested, but maybe you boys would like to try to find the house while you're here. It's a bit silly, and obviously not the sort of thing you usually do. But it might be challenging because it involves not only finding the house but the man who lived in it over twenty years ago. Maybe he still lives there, but I kind of doubt it."

Pete was skeptical. It seemed to him The Three Investigators would be better off investigating the bad things that had happened to Dr. Paxton – or even the protesters from OUTLAW – than biking around Sonoma looking for a house. But Pete could see that Jupiter was thinking hard; he pinched his lower lip.

"I believe we can take this on," Jupiter said. "We'll certainly give it a try. After all, we investigate anything."

"Wonderful," Dr. Paxton said. "I'm very grateful."

Pete wasn't at all sure it would be wonderful, but if Jupe and Bob were in, well, then, of course he was in too.

Jupiter took the Xeroxes from Phillipa Paxton and handed them to Bob.

"He'll keep them safe, Dr. Paxton," Jupiter said. "He's Records and Research. I hope we'll have good news for you in a day or so. In the meantime, you should call the number at the bottom of our card – Bob's cellphone number – if you think of something else you want to tell us."

Dr. Paxton took the card Jupiter handed her. The card read:

THE THREE INVESTIGATORS
"We Investigate Anything"
???
First Investigator – Jupiter Jones
Second Investigator – Pete Crenshaw
Records and Research – Bob Andrews

At the bottom was the new website address of their firm, the number of the landline in Headquarters, and the number of Bob's cellphone.

"Thank you, Jupiter," Dr. Paxton said. "Thanks to all of you. I'll look forward to seeing you again soon."

After saying goodbye to Pete's father, she put her messenger bag across her shoulder and strode off.

"Boys," Mr. Crenshaw said. "That's plenty of excitement for the time being. I think we ought to get settled in at the motel."

Pete thought that was a good idea. As

soon as they were settled, they could get to work, and while Jupiter's priority might be a house hunt, Pete's was going to be Daniel Hernández. He remembered the man's handshake and all-too-familiar manner, and he was itching to uncover what lay behind that overly-friendly smile.

6

Fire In The Hole!

Ten minutes later, Jupiter was sitting in the back seat of Mr. Crenshaw's truck, and as they headed to the motel, Jupiter was also thinking about Daniel Hernández. Mostly, he was wondering how he would have reacted if he hadn't been told in advance that Pete's father thought he wasn't to be trusted. It was an interesting question, really – and not just in this single instance, but in life in general. How much did what you'd been told about someone affect the way you reacted when you met him? It probably affected you a lot, Jupiter reflected.

However, in the case of Daniel Hernández, Jupiter was fairly certain that he would have disliked him whether or not he'd been told about him in advance. He also thought he'd have been at least a bit suspicious about his attitude toward OUTLAW. In fact, he *was* suspicious. While Hernández had tried to seem neutral about their presence, he'd been unable to conceal his delight that the protest group had shown up on the set.

Indeed, it seemed to Jupiter that OUT-

LAW was somehow serving Hernández's personal interests or ambitions. But how, exactly? In general, there was nothing about a mob that would seem to serve anyone or anything except the mob itself. Of course, Jupiter had never understood the lure of becoming part of a group like that. Why would anyone want to sacrifice their individual will to the shifting and dangerous whims of a mindless crowd?

And crowds, Jupiter thought, really *were* mindless. There was a madness about them that was frightening, and that frequently led to very bad outcomes.

But while that was true enough, it was really a separate consideration from the question of Daniel Hernández, Jupiter thought. In his case, the question was what did he have to gain, personally, from the presence of OUT-LAW on the set?

Well, for one thing, the negative publicity they were generating for Philippa Paxton's book was turning into positive publicity for Daniel Hernández's. And while Jupiter had always had *almost* as much trouble understanding that kind of opportunism as he had understanding the lure of a crowd, he supposed that for a man like Hernández, positive publicity for his book might be enough of a reason to do just about *anything*. Perhaps it was just his sheer, ruthless ambition he was trying to hide through his ingratiating manner, Jupiter thought.

But as Pete's father wove through heavy traffic toward the Wine Country Motel and Suites – which the cast and crew of *Bear Valley* had more or less taken over for the duration of the Sonoma shoot – he and Pete started talking about Phillipa Paxton.

Jupiter had been surprised when the mystery Dr. Paxton had asked The Three Investigators to solve wasn't about the ripped posters and slashed tires – the things Charlotte Mitchell had told them about the other night – but about something apparently irrelevant. He'd gotten the sense that either she, too, had been trying to hide something, or that this was a test of The Three Investigators' skills. If they passed the test, perhaps she would entrust them with something more important.

Whether or not Jupiter was right about that, now that The Three Investigators had taken on the case of the missing quilt, they had a responsibility to try to solve it – which meant finding one particular house in a perfect sea of houses. And since this sort of challenge had come up once or twice before, the moment

Phillipa Paxton had explained what she wanted, Jupiter had thought that now might be the perfect time to try an updated version of the Ghost-to-Ghost Hookup.

The original Ghost-to-Ghost Hookup – named after the Coast-to-Coast Hookup, a long-ago term describing a telephone call made from the East Coast to the West Coast – had been quite successful on several past occasions. When The Three Investigators had been on the lookout for something – a particular car, say – they had each called five friends who had then called five other friends and so on. This time, they would use e-mail, and this time, instead of each of them making their contacts separately, they would together make a list of everyone they could think of who might be willing to forward their e-mail on to other people.

At the motel, Mr. Crenshaw had reserved two rooms on the second floor with balconies and a connecting door, and while he went to check in and get the keys, Jupiter, Pete, and Bob took their bikes out of the truck and locked them to the bike rack. They grabbed their bags, caught up with Mr. Crenshaw, and followed him up to the suite. Each of the two rooms had two double beds, Jupiter saw. Pete and his father would share one room, while Jupiter and Bob shared the other.

As soon as the door was opened, Pete leaped up on the bed which was to be his — in the process almost hitting his head on the ceiling.

"Boy!" he yelled. "This is so great."

Mr. Crenshaw began laughing. "Stop it, Pete." He turned to Bob and Jupiter. "He's done that ever since he was little."

"I love motels!" Pete said, jumping back down.

Jupiter was glad that Pete was happy, but he was also itching to get started on implementing his idea. As soon as his friends had unpacked and settled in, he called them together and explained.

"Bob can take a picture of the photograph Dr. Paxton gave us," he said, "and we can attach it to an e-mail. We'll ask everyone who gets it to forward it on."

"That's a great idea!" Pete said. "And it sure beats riding up and down a lot of streets staring at houses. But we don't know anyone in Sonoma."

"I don't think that will be a problem," Jupiter said. "People move all the time these days, and I believe we'll spread a wide net very quickly. Also, I think we should send the e-mail to adults as well as to kids – maybe to adults we've met on some of our past cases."

"We could send it to Connor O'Malley and Gordon Small," Pete suggested.

"And to Hector Sebastian and Charlotte Mitchell," Bob said thoughtfully. "Maybe we could promise to put the names of any helpers into our next case report. After all, in the past, we've offered a reward to anyone who helped us."

"Excellent ideas," said Jupiter, nodding in approval. "Why don't you write the letter, Bob?"

Before he did that, Bob took a picture of the newspaper photo, then uploaded it to his laptop. After that, he wrote a draft of the letter, then gave it to Jupiter. Jupiter read it very carefully – checking for typos, making sure he could be proud of what was going out under the firm's name. Several months before, Bob had devised an electronic letterhead featuring their question marks, and Jupiter liked the way it looked.

When all three of them were satisfied that the letter was as good as they could make it, Bob attached the photograph he had taken, connected it to all the e-mail addresses they'd decided on, and pressed "Send."

For a moment, Jupiter stared avidly at the firm's IN box; irrationally, he hoped responses would soon come flooding in. But Bob had other ideas.

"We ought to shut down the laptop until tomorrow," Bob said. "By then we can be sure to have gotten responses, but right now we're wasting time."

"'A watched pot never boils,'" Jupiter agreed glumly. He had to admit that time seemed to stop when you were waiting for something to happen. He wished, and not for the first time, that he wasn't so obsessive. His nature was useful when intense concentration might yield results, but at other times it was simply annoying.

"So what should we do with the rest of the afternoon?" he asked.

"Let's take our bikes and explore," Bob said. "We hardly even got to look around the plaza. Then we can come back and have a swim."

They said goodbye to Mr. Crenshaw, then wound lazily down the streets of Sonoma. Though Jupiter gave every house they passed a second look, the one they were searching for was nowhere to be seen. They found West Spain Street, and it was a straight shot to the plaza.

After the ride in, Jupiter's shirt stuck to his back, and all three of them were hot and thirsty. They locked their bikes to a rack in the park at the plaza's center, then bought Italian ices from a street vendor and rested under the spreading trees on a bench opposite City Hall.

Jupiter surveyed the walking paths, which were crowded with tourists – most of them with young families. Mothers and fathers pushed strollers; irritable children, flushed from the heat, were protesting. Jupiter understood. It was hot. And aside from the heat, Jupiter was a terrible tourist at the best of times, and right now he had not just one but two mysteries on his mind – the more pressing being the elusive and suspicious Daniel Hernández.

Pete suggested they duck inside the coolness of the Sonoma Valley Visitors Bureau, where a young woman who was probably a college student working for the summer offered them some brochures. She suggested they see the Blue Wing Inn, a hotel and saloon from the 19th century; the monument to the Bear Flag Revolt; and the Mission San Francisco Solano, which was right across from the Sonoma Barracks.

By mistake she handed Pete a brochure

for the tasting room of a local winery at the far corner of the plaza, and then took it back.

"I don't think you're old enough," she said.

"We're almost fourteen," Pete said.

"That's what I meant," the girl said. "Have a nice day."

The whole time they trudged from one end of the plaza to the other, Jupiter's mind teemed with thoughts about the encounters with Dr. Hernández and Dr. Paxton. If Mr. Crenshaw's intuition was right – and so far, Jupiter had seen no reason to doubt that it was – it would require a subtle approach to uncover what Hernández was up to, and for the moment Jupiter was more interested in thinking about Dr. Paxton.

To Jupiter, she had seemed a very straightforward person – the sort of person who would choose to keep wearing the boots and hats and other clothes she had grown up wearing in Wyoming, even though she was now a college professor in southern California – and although he hadn't seen much of her yet, Jupiter had liked her. He hoped they could help her – and not just with the missing quilt!

In any case, by now Jupiter was so hot his friends had no trouble convincing him to ride back to the motel and take a swim. After they did, Mr. Crenshaw ordered Tex-Mex takeout and they ate tacos and burritos at a table in their room. They decided to make an early night of it. They wanted to get a good night's sleep. Tomorrow was the day they were going to watch the filming of the Bear Flag Revolt – and also try their best to do some sleuthing.

The next morning, Jupiter was anxious to check the firm's e-mail – though he did his best to appear nonchalant. He was gratified to see responses flood in, but also irritated to see that no one who'd responded had even bothered to change the subject heading.

Connor O'Malley had written to say that he'd forwarded the request on to everyone he knew. A number of people who'd gotten forwarded messages wrote to say they couldn't help, but good luck!

"'Dear Three Investigators,'" Bob read. "'Thank you for the interesting e-mail.'" He closed it and opened another one. "'I saw a house that sort of looked like this one – '" He sighed and opened another one.

All in all, they'd gotten over forty e-mails, and Jupiter was beginning to doubt that any of them would be helpful when Bob started reading again.

"'Dear The Three Investigators,'" he said. "'I am happy to tell you that I know where the house you are looking for is. I know because I am living in it.'"

"Wow!" Pete said. He'd been lying on the bed and he shot to his feet.

Jupiter sat up ramrod straight, smiling.

The house was indeed in the town of Sonoma, as Phillipa Paxton had thought. The boy who lived in the Arts and Crafts house with the unusual central chimney gave them the address and told them he'd be home that afternoon. If they wanted to come by, he'd show it to them. Bob had some trouble pronouncing the boy's name, though.

"I've never seen a first name like this," he said. "It's spelled B-r-a-n-k-o. Branko Petrovic."

Jupiter looked over Bob's shoulder at the screen. His senses were vibrating, but for an unexpected reason. Although Jupiter had been a baby when his parents had died, his mother had been Serbian, and Jupiter was pretty sure Branko Petrovic was a Serbian name. Bob looked it up online, and Jupiter was gratified to find out that he'd been right. The first name was pronounced like "bronco," and the "c" at the end of Petrovic was pronounced "ch". Branko Petrovic.

With Jupiter and Pete helping, Bob wrote two quick e-mails – one to everyone who'd written back, giving them the good news, and another to Branko, thanking him for writing and saying that they were looking forward to seeing him later, at about 4:00.

After a speedy breakfast, Mr. Crenshaw put the boys' bikes in the back of the truck. He'd be busy on set until 7:00 that evening, and after the main scene was filmed, and the boys did what they could to observe anything overtly suspicious, they planned to bike to Branko's house. They checked the address and found that it would take about twenty minutes to bicycle there from the Sonoma Barracks. After meeting Branko, they'd ride back and meet Pete's father at an outdoor café near the central plaza.

Mr. Crenshaw parked near the plaza and the boys secured their bikes. As they rounded the corner and crossed the park, Jupiter saw that the police had erected a second perimeter – another ring of sawhorses with yellow tape connecting them – effectively pushing the protesters further back and away.

OUTLAW was out in force this morning; to

Jupiter there seemed to be twice as many protesters as there had been the day before. They carried picket signs and poster boards; they struck their fists against the empty sky. Today they weren't yelling about "naiveté"; they were shouting "Silence Is Violence," and "Freedom Isn't Frémont!"

Aside from his instinctive dislike of crowds and mobs, Jupiter was also genuinely puzzled by OUTLAW's presence. What did they hope to accomplish by picketing this movie? Even if they managed to shut it down – a big *if*, but not impossible – all it would prove was that they didn't know their history.

After all, the Mexicans had been harassing, hounding, and killing the indigenous tribes for years before the American settlers arrived, and at the time of the Bear Flag Revolt, there had only been five hundred Americans in California, while there had been twelve thousand Mexicans. If OUTLAW really thought the local Indian tribes would have been better off if the land had stayed under Mexican rule, they were totally – well – naive.

Mr. Crenshaw ushered the boys around the barricades, behind the cameras and sound technicians, getting them a good spot from which to watch the actual filming – and anything else that might happen!

Now, the director was pacing, conferring with actors and cameramen, checking with a woman who sat up high at the end of a crane with a camera that would capture shots from above. Horse wranglers unloaded beautiful chestnut-brown stallions from horse trailers, and Jupiter could see the extras, dressed in 19th-century garb, wearing boots and chaps and colorful shirts and bandanas. Everywhere he looked there was movement and color and sound. Pete nudged him and pointed when two actors unfurled a replica of the original Bear Flag and attached its grommets to the flag-pole's halyard.

Since Jupiter himself had had a thankfully short-lived career as a child actor, he wasn't surprised to see how long everything was taking on the set. All the cameras and sound equipment needed to be carefully positioned; the actors needed to be made up, costumed, and put in their places; the horses needed to be saddled and bridled and calmed.

It was past noon when the filming began. The assistant director yelled for quiet and a hush fell over the plaza; Jupiter was glad to see that the protesters were sufficiently far away as to be both silent and invisible.

Just as always happened, a man came out with a clapperboard, announced the scene and the take, slapped the clapper, and the cameras started rolling. Jupiter watched as a small scrum of men on horseback, pistols on their hips, rode up before the barracks. Dust swirled; horses neighed. The men tied their mounts to the hitching post and stealthily approached the barracks door. Jupiter looked at his friends. Pete had a big smile on his face and Bob looked very intent. That was all very well, but neither of them seemed to be paying much attention to what be going on *behind* the scenes – though that was the real point of their being here today.

Now, one of the actors threw his shoulder against the door and it flew open. In no time, the American settlers came back outside with a man Jupiter assumed was the Mexican commander, Vallejo.

"Cut!" the director shouted.

Mr. Crenshaw and his crew ran to return the set to its earlier condition as the actors retreated for another take. The action itself had lasted only a few minutes.

Jupiter watched as they shot the same scene four more times. While they did, he tried his best to keep his eye on things. Twice, he got up and walked around to see what was happening just outside of camera range. Not much, from what he could tell. It was strange how vividly being on this set brought back his early acting experiences.

But although most of what he remembered was pretty unpleasant, it had actually proved an oddly good start to his life. In the first place, even now, he frequently drew on his early training to act stupider than he really was. He had a trick of letting his eyes grow dull and his face go slack which had fooled a surprising number of bad guys.

In the second place, there was nothing like acting to bring home the difference between appearance and reality. Phonies like Daniel Hernández took advantage of that difference all the time.

But although Jupiter had been looking for Hernández ever since they'd gotten to the set, not only had he not seen him, he hadn't even seen Phillipa Paxton. This was a disappointment, since he had hoped to be able to tell her in person about Branko Petrovic's letter. Should he borrow Bob's cellphone and call her? Jupiter wondered. Maybe he should.

Luckily, just then, Dr. Paxton appeared – and when she saw Jupiter, she waved at him vigorously, at which he got to his feet and joined her. By now, behind him, the film crew had moved on to film the scene of the settlers raising the Bear Flag, but Dr. Paxton was looking at nothing but Jupiter, and when he joined her, he was surprised to see that she looked very upset – on the verge of tears.

"Dr. Paxton," he said. "What's wrong? Is there something I can do? I was just thinking of calling you to give you the good news. We seem to have found the house you're looking for, and we have an appointment to go there this afternoon."

At this news, Phillipa Paxton's face was totally transformed.

"Why, Jupiter. That's wonderful. And in-credible. Truly incredible. Well, not *actually* in-credible – since that means too extraordinary to be believed, and I *do* believe it. How did you do it?"

"Through something we call a Ghost-to-Ghost Hookup," Jupiter said. He briefly ex-plained the concept, then asked again what was wrong.

"Something stupid," Phillipa Paxton said. "Or maybe not. I put my messenger bag down for a minute, and now it's missing. I know I put it on that box over there, but nobody seems to have seen it. The thing is, this isn't the first time something like this has happened. If I'd been honest with you yesterday, I'd have said that if you *really* wanted to investigate something, you could start with all the strange and disturbing things that have happened to me recently."

"Charlotte mentioned some of them the other night at Isabella Chang's," Jupiter said

Phillipa looked pleased to hear this. "Charlotte is really a love," she said. "Yes, well, when I went to my office at the college about a week ago I found that someone had trashed my door. I'd put up a poster about the movie and someone had spray-painted CANCELED on it. They'd also ripped up a copy of the book jacket of *Bear Valley* I had taped there. Then, several days later, I went out to the parking lot after work to find that someone had slashed two of my tires, trying to make it look like I'd run over a beer bottle without noticing it. But clearly the glass had been put there afterwards."

"That sounds pretty serious," Jupiter said. "Some people would have called the police."

"I know," Dr. Paxton said. "But I didn't want to make a fuss and attract attention. I

132

just hoped some crazy had acted impulsively, and the whole thing would stop. But then someone, or some group, started trolling me online as well. I've always prided myself on being a good teacher, and my evaluations on those sites that rate professors have always been positive. But suddenly all sorts of anonymous people were posting vicious and false comments about me, and rating me as low as possible – which caused my overall rating to drop terribly. It really hurt my feelings."

"It sounds like organized harassment," Jupiter said. "I assume you think that OUTLAW is responsible."

Dr. Paxton sent a baleful glance in the direction of the protesters in the distance.

"Since it all started not long after OUTLAW began its social media campaign against this movie, I *do* think they're behind it," she said. "And now they've stolen my messenger bag!"

Just then a young man came up behind them; he seemed to be a member of the film crew.

As they turned toward him, Jupiter saw Daniel Hernández strolling toward a place at the edge of the set. He tried to keep his eyes on him but the young man was in the way.

"Dr. Paxton," the young man said. "Is this yours?"

Dr. Paxton looked both overjoyed and slightly embarrassed. "My messenger bag!" she said. "Thank you so much, Sam. I thought it was lost."

"No problem," he said. He smiled and returned to his work.

Dr. Paxton opened the bag and checked through it to make sure nothing was missing. Jupiter was straining to see, but he'd lost track of Daniel Hernández.

"Well," said Dr. Paxton. "*That's* a huge relief. I guess I got all worked up over nothing. Still, if anything else happens on this other front" – she gestured with her head in the direction of OUTLAW – "I'll get in touch with you right away."

She had barely finished speaking when the air was forcefully rent by an explosion. Even at this distance Jupiter could feel the force of the air the explosion had displaced. People screamed. Dr. Paxton gasped. Jupiter's first thought was to check on Pete and Bob – who he was relieved to quickly find in the crowd, not too far away. Everyone was pointing and talking, staring in disbelief.

As the smoke cleared, Jupiter was

shocked to see an actor in the costume of a Mexican soldier sprawled on the street. Several people ran up to him, and though the man had looked dead or unconscious, he wasn't. Apparently he'd been knocked off his feet by the shock of the explosion – but the explosion itself had done little damage. With the help of the people who'd come to his aid, the actor got up and dusted himself off.

The crowd of onlookers stared in confusion. Jupiter was sure that all special effects on the set had been coordinated and checked so that nothing like this could happen. He craned his neck to see better, but security guards and police had arrived. It didn't take long for the word to spread that someone had ignited a wooden keg containing a small amount of real gunpowder.

No one could figure out how this could have happened; the props people swore that the only kegs they'd placed around the plaza had been empty. Certainly no one on crew could have been this brainless or careless, so Jupiter quickly reached the conclusion that this had been no accident – that someone had deliberately brought and positioned the keg and ignited the gunpowder. Since all the protesters had been kept far away from the set, it couldn't have been one of them. Jupiter wondered if he'd been right when he'd thought that OUT-LAW might have planted someone on the crew of *Bear Valley*.

If so, how could he find out who it was? Maybe there was a clue of some sort on OUT-LAW's Facebook page. He and the others could study it tonight. Mr. Crenshaw clearly hadn't been wrong when he told The Three Investigators that something was amiss on the set of *Bear Valley*, and Jupiter had the uncomfortable feeling that it might not be as easy to figure out what that *something* was as it had been to get a bead on the Arts and Crafts house with the striking central chimney.

7

The Serbian Connection

As Bob pedaled away from the plaza and the town center, the traffic thinned and the general noise level decreased. That was fine with Bob; between the filming and the explosion, he'd had enough drama for the moment. He hadn't imagined that a group like OUTLAW would do something like blow up a barrel of gunpowder.

Even now, he wasn't sure they had. Sometimes people in protest marches got swept away by emotion and ended up damaging walls and cars and storefronts, but this was different. It seemed planned. He'd be interested to hear what Pete and Jupiter thought about it when they had the chance to talk.

In the meantime, Bob was using the firm's GPS to navigate to Branko Petrovic's house. Their route took them down quiet residential streets. Many of the houses were substantial, with circular pebble driveways and extensive plantings. After riding for about fifteen minutes, Bob could see that they were getting close.

"Make a left at the STOP sign," he

called, "and Branko's house should be the third one on the right."

The three boys brought their bikes to a halt and stared at the house. Bob got out the photo that Dr. Paxton had given them. It sure enough looked like the same house. A newish stone wall edged a perennial border of native grasses, and there were vines now entwined along the length of the portico. But the lines of the redwood-shingled house were identical, as was the unmistakable central chimney. Bob was surprised to see a large FOR SALE sign on the lawn, a banner across it reading SOLD.

"Branko didn't say anything about that," Bob said. "It looks like we got here just in time. This has to be the place."

The boys left their bikes under some bushes and walked up the long stone path to the front door. Bob was not used to admiring doors, but this one was extraordinary. It had six windows at the top, and was made of redwood which glowed as if it had been polished. Their knock was swiftly answered.

The door flew open and a boy their age, maybe just a touch older, stood there, an expectant expression on his face. He was as tall as Pete − lean, muscular, and wiry, with a taut face, gleaming eyes, and a helmet of bristly black hair. He had an electric air about him, as though he might fly off in any one of a number of different directions.

"The Three Investigators?" he said in accented English. It was an accent Bob had never heard before, though it almost sounded Russian.

"Yes," Jupiter said. "And you're Branko Petrovic. Did I pronounce your name right?"

"Very well!" Branko said. "Come in, please." He stepped backwards, bowed low, and swept his arm before him. When he closed the door, he revealed a younger boy and girl who had been hiding behind it. "This is my sister Milena and my brother Zivko. They will not bother us too much."

Both Milena and Zivko had dark hair, like their brother. Milena's was shoulder-length, braided and plaited with a red ribbon. Zivko had a buzz cut, and his hair stuck out about a half inch all over his head. While Branko had a manner approaching formality, the younger children were giggly and shy.

"I'm taking care of them until our parents come home," Branko said. "Go play now," he said sternly, and Milena and Zivko ran off, bounding and shouting.

Branko shook his head in apology.

"They are ten and eleven," he explained.

The boys stood awkwardly for a moment or so; no one knew what to say next. Finally Branko broke the silence. "So you are in Sonoma to look for my house?"

Pete laughed. "Not really," he said. "My dad is working on that movie they're shooting downtown – "

"*Bear Valley*," Branko said. "Very cool."

"And we're actually here to investigate trouble on the set," Jupiter said. "Finding your house was a – "

Bob could see Jupiter didn't know how to complete the sentence.

" – another mystery," Bob said. "It was really nice of you to answer our e-mail."

"I love mysteries," Branko said, smiling for the first time. "And I was excited to meet three detectives who are my own age." He paused and looked bashful. "You will have to pardon my English, please."

"Not at all," Jupiter said. "Your English is excellent."

"I grew up in Serbia," Branko said. "But I studied English there, and we moved to America five years ago."

"And it looks like you're moving again," Bob said.

"Yes," Branko said. "We had a vineyard in Serbia, in the Timok valley. My parents worked very hard and our wine became so well-known my father was asked to come to this country to manage a vineyard near Sonoma. Then he got a better job at another vineyard in the town of Jackson."

"Jackson!" Pete said. "Why, we were just there a few weeks ago."

"There are many Serbians in Jackson," Branko said. "They came to look for gold and stayed. That is where we are moving. When my father's boss decided to retire, he offered to sell the vineyard to my father. The new vineyard became ours around Christmas, but Papa wanted to wait to move there until the school year was over."

While they talked, Branko took them through to the kitchen. Bob was very impressed with how welcoming the house was − not ostentatious or showy, but warm, and comfortable and nice. The rooms had wood wainscoting and polished wood floors with hand-woven rugs; the dining room had three wide floor-to-ceiling windows − one of which doubled as a door. It was clear that Branko's parents were wealthy, but what really struck Bob about their house (and their children) was that they were openhearted.

In the kitchen Branko said, "Would you like some orange juice?"

Bob looked up to see Milena and Zivko standing in the doorway.

"You can have some, too," said Branko. "But no cookies!"

Bob thought that Branko was a very good older brother, and he wished, not for the first time, that he'd had a sibling or two. He was very glad to have friends like Jupiter and Pete − who were actually more like brothers than friends.

Branko carefully poured six small glasses of juice and put out a plate of cookies. He glared at Zivko, just in case his brother hadn't heard his earlier admonition. The two younger children sat on stools, swinging their legs with more enthusiasm than was strictly necessary, but they kept quiet. As Bob helped himself to a cookie, he noticed that Pete, who was never shy when it came to "refreshments," was refraining. Perhaps he'd eaten too much at the buffet.

Pete took a sip of his juice. "You're the very first Serbian I've ever met," he said. "It's kind of cool, because Jupiter's mother was Serbian."

Branko turned to Jupiter. "Really?" he said. "Is this so?"

"Yes," Jupiter said. "It's true, though I don't know anything about her. She and my father died when I was still a baby, and you're the first Serbian I've ever met, too."

"So when are you moving?" Pete asked.

"In three days," Zivko shouted.

"O.K.," Branko said. "That's enough. Now, off with the two of you. Play quietly and Mama and Papa will be back soon." He turned to Pete.

"Yes, he said. "As Zivko said, we are moving in three days. It is only two hours from here to Jackson and we've all been going up every weekend. But we've talked enough about me. Why did you want to find this house?"

Jupiter explained about Dr. Paxton, the newspaper photograph, and the flag quilt she was looking for. He went on to say that the house was merely a way station on their search. Next they had to discover the name of the man who had lived here in 1998 and then to try to find him.

"Now that we're sure this is the same house as the one in the photograph," Bob said, "I'll probably be able to get online and

143

search the property records."

"That should not be necessary," Branko said, "because I know the name of the man who lived here. Come, I'll show you."

Bob was quite excited as the three boys followed Branko along a hall, through a door, and down a flight of stairs. Branko flipped a switch and a few lights hanging by cords from the ceiling flashed on. It was dry in the basement, and both dim and dusty, but Bob's eyes adjusted as he followed Branko across a stone floor to a large cabinet made of light wood. It had a lot of drawers, each about three inches high, across the bottom, and two rows of narrower but higher drawers above that. The top was glass-fronted and had shelves behind the doors.

"This looks like a collector's cabinet," Bob said.

"I think it was," said Branko. He opened the very bottom drawer and pulled out a sheaf of papers. He offered them to Jupiter, but Jupiter said, "You should give them to Bob. He's Records and Research," and in no time, Bob was leafing through them.

Bob found catalogues from auction houses, pages torn from newspapers, a few magazine articles with pages stapled together, and various papers with almost indecipherable handwriting, a small crabbed hand in pencil. But there were also, he was excited to see, a number of invoices for items that had belonged to the collector.

Whose name turned out to be John Smith.

Bob groaned.

"What's the matter?" Pete asked.

"Oh, nothing," Bob said. "Only that the name of the man we're looking for happens to be John Smith. There must be over five thousand John Smiths in California. If he's even still here. He could have moved anywhere. And Smith is the most common name all over the United States."

For some reason Pete thought this was very funny.

"That is a problem," Jupiter said. "We'll need to find a way to narrow down the possibilities."

"Do you think we could get copies of some of these invoices?" Bob asked Branko.

"You can have them," Branko said. "I am happy to be able to help The Three Investigators."

They trudged back up the stairs, and as they were walking toward the kitchen, the front door opened and a man and a woman came into the house. As if they'd been alerted by a psychic force, Milena and Zivko stampeded into the hall and hugged their parents.

Branko beckoned to Bob and his friends. "Mama, Papa," he said. "These are the boys I told you about, The Three Investigators. This is Pete Crenshaw, and Jupiter Jones, and Bob Andrews."

Mrs. Petrovic was a petite woman with dark blue eyes. She smiled at the boys as she shook their hands.

"Welcome," she said. "It is so nice to meet you. We're always happy to meet Branko's friends."

Mr. Petrovic was tall and broad-shouldered, tan from his work in the vineyards, and well-muscled. His hands were large and weathered.

"We are so glad you could come," he said. "Are you hungry? We must eat. Jelena, we have food in the refrigerator, no?"

"Of course," Branko's mother said. "I have gibanica and cabbage rolls all ready, and I will make some chevapi and potatoes, if you can stay for dinner."

"These boys would probably like something a little more all-American," said Mr.

Petrovic.

"Jupiter's mother was Serbian," Branko said.

A look of interest crossed Mr. Petrovic's face. "Is that so?" he asked. Jupiter quickly explained that he lived with his Aunt Mathilda and his Uncle Titus, and that he had never known his parents. They were a mystery to him.

"Still, you must stay for dinner," Mr. Petrovic responded.

Normally Pete would have been jumping for joy, so Bob thought it was amusing when he said they couldn't stay.

"Thank you very much, but we had a big lunch not long ago, and we're supposed to be meeting my father for dinner in a little while."

"That is too bad," Mrs. Petrovic said, "but some other time, then."

"Yes," Mr. Petrovic said. "You must come to visit us in our new home as soon as we are settled."

Bob was astonished at their warmth and hospitality.

"That is very kind of you," Jupiter said. "But –"

"We insist. Branko will show you how to work in the vineyard."

"Papa!" Branko said.

"I'm only joking," his father said. "Ha *ha!*"

Branko smiled, and he and his father bumped fists.

"He is a comedian," Branko said. "But you must come. I have enjoyed meeting all three of you very much."

Bob looked at Pete and Jupiter and noticed that Jupiter seemed quite relaxed – something rare in social events of this sort.

In fact, it seemed to Bob that Jupe liked Branko in a way he rarely liked strangers whose acquaintance he had just made. Bob couldn't help but wish that he would show the same open-mindedness with Mallory MacLeod – especially when he saw the way Jupiter reacted to what got said next.

"And you, young man," Mr. Petrovic said, looking at Jupiter. "When you come, you will meet other Serbs, and we will have a celebration. There is much you need to know about your heritage. We will drink to your health – a glass of wine will not hurt you – and dance the kolo."

Under normal circumstances, Jupiter would have run from such an invitation, but now he was nodding as if he would actually

148

look forward to it. Bob couldn't wait to see Jupiter dance the kolo.

They thanked the Petrovics for their kindness and said they looked forward to seeing them again. Then Branko walked them down the path to where they had hidden their bikes.

"This is good," Branko said. "I am happy to have met you. I hope you really will be able to visit us at the vineyard."

"I hope so, too," said Jupiter warmly. He shook Branko's hand, and then they all retrieved their bikes, strapped on their helmets, and took off.

The route was not difficult, and Bob simply ran it in reverse; he didn't need the GPS this time. When they reached the café where they'd agreed to meet Pete's father, the boys found an outdoor table where they ordered something to drink while they waited for Mr. Crenshaw. They looked again at the copies of the articles and invoices Branko had found.

No new clues surfaced, even when Bob studied the material at leisure; the name John Smith appeared again and again, but there was no information about who he was, or what he did – or even how old he was.

The boys were so engrossed in studying

the papers that they were startled when Pete's father pulled up a chair and joined them. He looked wide-eyed, even vigilant. Bob immediately knew something was up.

"What's the matter?" Pete asked his father.

"As if that explosion wasn't enough commotion for one day," Mr. Crenshaw said. "After you left, there was more trouble. The OUTLAW crowd kept getting bigger and louder and more unruly, and at one point, a small bunch of them knocked over a barricade and managed to evade both the cops and the security men. They got their hands on the prop Bear Flag and American flag, doused them with gas, and set them on fire."

"Holy moly!" Pete said. "Was anyone hurt?"

"Unfortunately, yes," Mr. Crenshaw said. "When the cops turned their attention to the flag burners, other OUTLAWs joined the fight, and things got pretty rough. A young thug seemed to target Dr. Paxton – "

"Oh, no!" Jupiter said.

" – and shoved her so hard she fell and cut her leg. He was screaming 'No invaders here!' if you can believe it." He shook his head in disgust.

"Is she O.K.?" Bob asked.

"Yes," Mr. Crenshaw said, "though she had to get stitches at the medical tent. The police arrested the guy and found a garrote in his backpack."

"A garrote!" Jupiter said.

"What's that?" Pete said, looking from his father to Jupiter.

"It's a piece of cloth or wire with a handle on each end," Jupiter said, "that you use to strangle someone."

"Yikes!" Pete said.

"You can say that again," Jupiter said. "In 17th- and 18th-century India, garrotes were used by the Thuggee cult to assassinate people, but I've never heard of them being used at a protest march."

Just at that moment Bob's cellphone rang, and when he looked around the table, the others urged him to pick up.

"Hello?" he said. "This is Bob Andrews."

The voice on the other end was distraught. "Bob, this is Phillipa Paxton."

"Dr. Paxton!" Bob said, looking at the others who now stared at him intently. "Mr. Crenshaw just told us what happened. Are you all right?"

"Yes and no," Dr. Paxton said.

"Because of what happened, I'm heading back to Rocky Beach this evening, and I'm calling to ask if you and Jupiter and Pete would be good enough to come see me once you're back as well. I'd like to consult with you."

Bob covered the mouthpiece and told the others what Dr. Paxton had said.

"Of course," Jupiter said. "Make an appointment for the day after tomorrow."

"We're driving back tomorrow," Bob said. "So we could come to see you the day after. Maybe late morning?"

"That sounds perfect," Dr. Paxton said. She gave Bob the address and he carefully wrote it down. "See you soon, then," she said. "Goodbye."

Bob hung up and looked at Jupiter and Pete. In his mind was an image of the young man he had seen storm the sawhorses in the plaza when the three of them had been nearby. Had he been the one with the garrote? Who was he? Why did he have a lethal weapon in his bag?

"I think," Jupiter said, "that we should head back to the motel so that we can scrutinize OUTLAW's Facebook page."

Mr. Crenshaw had some last minute work to take care of before he left again for

Rocky Beach, so the three of them biked back to the Wine Country Motel. There they gathered around Bob's laptop and studied pictures of OUTLAW members, their fists raised, their mouths in a snarl.

When people became part of a mob, anger was all they felt, Bob thought — anger that made them sure they were right and that those who opposed them were wrong. He looked for a picture of the man he presumed they had arrested and found one. There he was – his eyes gleaming as if he were a member of a cult.

There was also a new post by Honon Miwok which referred to a "fellow member who has just been arrested," and suggested that everyone contribute to a legal defense fund. At the end of that post was Phillipa Paxton's home address in Rocky Beach, and although no suggestion was made about what to do with the address, the mere fact that it had been posted on the Internet in this context seemed ominous to Bob.

That night, before the three of them went to bed, they sat on the balcony of the room Bob and Jupiter were sleeping in, listening to the sounds of children still playing around the swimming pool.

"These Internet mobs are really scary

when they go after someone," Bob found himself saying. "What they do is worse than actual violence; you can fight actual violence – or investigate it – but you can't fight an anonymous horde of vigilantes all trying to destroy the life of a single person."

"That's the word Mallory used, too," Pete said. "Vigilantes."

"Unfortunately, our ancestors evolved to demand allegiance to the codes of their in-group," Jupiter said, to the sound of splashing in the pool below.

"They evolved to do *what?*" Pete asked, stretching his legs out.

"They wanted to punish or evict those who didn't try hard enough to fit in," Jupiter explained. "Evolution made human beings tribal, and only recently have people begun to understand how destructive that can be."

He was silent for a while. "That's why it's so important to protect the rights of individuals over the rights of groups," he added.

"But we're a group," Pete said. "A group of three."

"That's right," Jupiter said. "Three individuals – all committed to investigating mysteries!"

8

An Important Deduction

It was two days later, and as Pete woke up to the sound of his father pounding on his bedroom door, he had a moment of confusion when he didn't know who or where he was. For a very brief instant, he felt panicked and imagined that the police were coming to arrest him for some forgotten crime. Though he was relieved when he remembered he was home in his own bed, he was also surprised at how alarmed he had felt.

He called out, "All right, Dad. I'm up now," then jumped into action – or at least into the shower. After which he scrambled into his clothes.

The day before, his father had driven himself and The Three Investigators back to Rocky Beach, and on the way, they'd stopped for lunch at a diner which had public Wi-Fi. Bob had brought his laptop into the diner and found an e-mail from Branko.

"Listen to this," Bob had said. "After we left, Branko asked his parents if they had a copy of the deed to the Sonoma house. He thought it might provide some more information – and when they looked at the deed, they found that the man who owned the house when the replica flag was there had a middle name. His full name is John Lysander Smith."

"Lysander?" Pete had asked.

After punching a few quick words into his search engine, Bob had said, "It isn't a very common name. Unlike Smith. In 2018, over six thousand male names were more common than Lysander. Out of six thousand and ten."

"That's great news," Jupiter had said. "A name that rare should get us a lot closer to the mystery of the missing flag quilt. You can research it soon, Bob, and see if you can find the man himself."

Now, as Pete got ready to help his father finish building a picnic table he'd been working on whenever he'd been home, he found himself thinking again what he had thought in the diner the day before: Who *cared* about that stupid flag quilt, anyway? What did it matter, really?

Sure, it had been nice to meet Branko and his younger siblings, but what seemed far more important to Pete than some old commemorative quilt was the question of what Daniel Hernández was up to on the set of *Bear Valley* – and why.

After all, what had already happened was really very serious. Not only had OUTLAW breached the barricades and burned an American flag, but one of the protesters — one carrying a garrote! — had attacked Dr. Paxton. What would happen next? Someone had already lit a keg of gunpowder on the set. What if someone brought a gun? What if someone tried to burn the place down? Anything could happen, really!

But beneath his worries Pete could not stop thinking about Daniel Hernández and what a slippery character he was. So slippery he sometimes disappeared from view entirely while explosions and black-clad protesters captured everyone's attention.

Pete remembered an old science fiction TV show he'd seen a couple of times on late night TV — a show in which the aliens looked just like regular human beings, though if you ripped off their skin, they were really lizards underneath.

That was it, Pete thought as he finished getting dressed. There was something reptilian about Daniel Hernández. Pete resolved not to lose track of the man who seemed to be hiding in the shadows. All of a sudden Pete remembered that just before his father had pounded on the door, he'd been having a dream in which a shadowy male figure, dressed in black and clearly an OUTLAW, was hiding in Pete's bedroom – the very bedroom he had been having the dream in – and laughing nastily at Pete.

But why? He couldn't quite remember *that*. Or could he? Had it been something about Daniel Hernández – about something he'd said? Or something he *hadn*'t said, perhaps? Yes, that was it, Pete thought. Or maybe. It was just on the tip of his mind now – but what *was* it?

From outside, in the back yard, he heard his father's voice.

"Up and at 'em, cowboy!" his father yelled. "I need your help. Grab some breakfast, then get your hammer!"

That was it! Pete thought triumphantly. It had something to do with his father and Daniel Hernández. Though *what*, he still didn't know.

Pete sprang to his feet and ran to the kitchen where his mother had left him breakfast. His mother was running errands at the moment, or he could have asked *her* what it was he couldn't quite remember. If nothing else, she could have consulted her Tarot cards or the I Ching!

Outside at last, Pete found that his father had already finished whacking the old picnic table apart with a sledgehammer and was waiting for Pete to help him assemble the new one. He'd been milling the pieces on and off for several weeks. Now they needed to fasten the whole thing together.

"Come hold this leg assembly," his father said.

Pete positioned it and kept it steady while his father bolted it, then drove a nail into a piece of metal. As he watched him pounding the nail, his fist wrapped around the handle of the hammer, Pete thought of the day his father had asked him and Bob if they'd like to come to Sonoma, along with Jupiter, to launch an investigation into what was going on there. He'd said that if he and Hernández had been in high school together, he'd have probably punched his lights out.

That was it! Pete thought. That was the thing he'd been trying to remember ever since he woke up. The thing that had been bothering him even when he was asleep. If his father really hated Daniel Hernández, why had he told him about The Three Investigators?

"Can I ask you something, Dad?" he said now.

"Sure," his father said. But the whine of his father's drill made talking impossible. Pete held the other leg assembly and waited for his father to take a break.

"There," his father said. "Now let's turn it over."

As they stood looking down on the finished table, Pete said, "I was wondering. If you really don't like Dr. Hernández, why did you tell him about me and Jupiter and Bob?"

"What do you mean?" his father asked. "Tell him what?"

"When we met him, he said you told him you were thinking of bringing us to the set," Pete explained. "And somehow he knew all about The Three Investigators – about the gold we found in Auburn, and other stuff too."

His father frowned. "Well, I certainly never told him any of that. We don't exchange small talk. In fact, I never talk to him at all if I can help it. Maybe he overheard me when I was talking to Richard Black, the director. I'm proud of what you and Bob and Jupiter have managed to do, and I was bragging a little. But I certainly wouldn't have told Hernández anything personal. I wouldn't trust him as far as I could throw him. And I'd like to throw him."

He grinned after he said this, but in a way that meant he was half-serious.

"He was really interested in us," Pete said. "And now I'm suddenly wondering why."

For a moment, Pete's father looked almost as worried as Pete had felt when he had woken up.

"You say Hernández had done research on The Three Investigators?" he asked.

"He sure had," Pete said. "Almost as if he was thinking that we might be coming to investigate *him*. He tried hard to get us to like him. It was pretty icky."

"Hmm," his father said. "In a way, maybe that's good. I have no idea why a guy like him would be wary of three teenagers. Still, my gut tells me he's a nasty piece of work, and since my gut also told me to bring The Three Investigators onto the case, maybe you're *just* the kind of investigators who can get to the bottom of whatever's actually going on!"

"Maybe we are!" said Pete. In fact, now, more than ever, he couldn't help but hope that his father's faith in The Three Investigators would prove to be well-founded. Though he could hardly believe it, he'd deduced something all on his own. He'd logically determined that his father and Daniel Hernández could not both be telling the truth. And he knew who *he* believed.

It was time for him to leave for the Salvage Yard, and soon he and Bob and Jupiter were on their bikes again – this time heading to Phillipa Paxton's house on the edge of town. On the way, Pete filled his friends in on his great deduction. He was glad when they seemed quite impressed.

"And I agree with your father," Jupiter added. "This is actually good news. Before, all we had was a vague and hinky feeling about Hernández. Now, we have something real. I wonder if Dr. Paxton will be able to shed more light on the Hernández situation."

As it turned out, Dr. Paxton's house was southwestern in style and seemed as though it belonged in Santa Fé rather than Rocky Beach. It had a red tile roof that slanted over the floor of the porch and was supported by wooden poles, and white adobe walls with dark-framed windows that rose to an arch. The front door was rustic and made of thick weathered wood.

Dr. Paxton answered the door wearing a skirt that let them see the bandage on her leg. Hobbling a bit, she brought them into her living room – both glad to see them and very agitated. Inside, the cool white walls were hung with weavings and photographs. There was a beehive fireplace in the corner.

"Please sit down," Dr. Paxton said. "I'm afraid I'm a bit of a mess. Things have gotten worse since I got back to Rocky Beach."

Worse! Pete thought. The other day she'd needed stitches! What could have happened that was worse?

"While I was up in Sonoma, someone broke into my office at the college and ransacked the place," Dr. Paxton went on. "On Tuesday morning, a janitor noticed that my door was slightly open and when he went in, he found papers everywhere. He called the campus police, who called the local police, and the place has been turned into a crime scene. Yellow tape, fingerprint dust."

"That's quite disturbing," Jupiter said.

"Yes it is," said Dr. Paxton. "And I'm afraid finding out who broke in will be hopeless. Students are in and out of my office all the time. There must be forty or fifty sets of fingerprints in there. The police won't find anything they can use."

Yikes! Pete thought. Up until this moment, all his worries had been confined to Sonoma.

"What do you think the burglars were looking for?" Bob asked.

"I have no idea," Dr. Paxton said. "But all my important papers – all my research and all my memorabilia – are here in my house, not my office. So their search was fruitless from the start. Unless they were looking for grade sheets or student evaluations."

Dr. Paxton looked haggard; it seemed she hadn't been sleeping, and when she mentioned that her husband was away for four weeks in London, Pete thought that that couldn't be helping.

Jupiter looked grave, but asked, "Is there anything else you can tell us?"

"I spent most of yesterday afternoon with the police at my office," she said, "and I told them what seems obvious to me – that OUTLAW must be behind what had happened. They agreed that that was probably the case but didn't think they could prove it."

"You said you didn't know what the vandals might have been after," Jupiter said. "So you assume the item is here, in your house?"

"Yes," Dr. Paxton said. "Everything of real value is here. I've been collecting memorabilia connected to the Frémonts for years, but

164

most of it is quite obscure. It'd be of little interest to anyone other than Frémont scholars. I
do have some papers of historical importance
and value – perhaps some of real value. I've
never had them appraised. I've got letters that
John and Jessie Frémont wrote and received,
and three letters to Frémont from Kit Carson."

"Kit Carson!" Pete said. "You have letters he wrote?"

"Well, Pete," Dr. Paxton said. "Since
Carson never learned to read or write, someone else wrote them for him. He signed them,
though. Would you like to see them?"

"Boy, would I!" Pete said.

Pete and the others followed Dr. Paxton
into her study. She opened a filing cabinet and
took out a sheaf of letters, each of them carefully placed inside a glassine envelope.

As she took one out, Bob said, "Don't
you need to wear white gloves?"

Phillipa shook her head. "A lot of people
think so, but no. Gloves actually make your
hands sweat, and they interfere with your sense
of touch, so it's easier to tear the paper or drop
it. Just make sure your hands are clean and be
careful."

She opened three different letters that
Kit Carson had written to John Frémont and

laid them on her desk to let the boys look at them. Despite what she'd said, none of them touched the paper.

Pete was intrigued to see the differences in the handwriting of the letters. All three had been written by people who had been with Carson at the time, but each was distinct. All three held the same signature, however.

"That's Kit Carson's signature," Dr. Paxton said. "His real name was Christopher, so he signed 'C Carson.'"

"I understand that John Frémont is the one who actually made Kit Carson famous," Bob said. "That he hired Carson as a guide on his expeditions and then wrote about him afterwards."

"Carson worked with people like Frémont," Dr. Paxton said, "but he was never really one of them. He'd think it really odd that people these days would pay to own one of his letters. And now that I think about it, that's another reason I dislike Daniel Hernández. He tried to persuade me to sell my Carson collection to him. He offered to buy it or to exchange it for items from *his* collection − whatever that is.

"I started collecting Frémont memorabilia not because I thought it might become valuable but because I liked it," Dr. Paxton added. "So Hernández's assumption that I was interested in money really annoyed me. At that point I'm afraid I acted badly. I told him quite snidely I sincerely doubted he had anything I'd be remotely interested in, and that I had no intention of parting with my collection."

"Would you lend us a copy of your book?" Jupiter asked suddenly.

"I'd be happy to give you one," she said. From a shelf in her study, she pulled down a hardcover volume, opened it, and wrote something on one of the first pages. She handed the book to Jupiter, who read aloud to all of them, "To The Three Investigators, who I expect will have a prodigious destiny of their own.'"

Pete was glad he now knew what "prodigious" meant.

"Thanks, Dr. Paxton," he said. "Thanks a lot."

Bob and Jupiter thanked her, too, and then she led the way back to the living room, shaking her head in dismay.

"I'm afraid this whole affair has really shaken me up," she said. "I've never felt threatened before. While I was on campus yesterday, I was talking to several other faculty members, and they told me that OUTLAW is actively re-

cruiting at area colleges and that students from
our own school have joined. I don't know which
ones; some may even have been my own students. They're everywhere now − at Daniel
Hernández's university, as well."

"He seemed to really like teaching when
we spoke to him," Pete said. "He told us how
much he enjoys talking to students in his
office."

"I bet he does," Dr. Paxton said. "The
better to fill their ears with poison."

Wow! Pete thought. Dr. Paxton could
join the Hernández Haters Club. "He knew all
about us," Pete said. "I mean The Three Investigators. He looked us up online. I thought
my dad must have told him we were coming to
the set, but he told me this morning he never
did. He must have overheard."

"That's another word for 'eavesdropping,'"
Jupiter said. "I didn't pay much attention to it
at the time, but it now seems fairly odd that a
grown man with no real connection to us would
have gone to the trouble to research our firm
so thoroughly. If I may ask, what else do you
know about Dr. Hernández?"

"Not all that much," Dr. Paxton said.
"I'd never heard of him until he showed up on
the set and introduced himself. He said he'd en-

joyed my book, which he'd gone out to buy after he read an article in a magazine about the movie. But really, he was extremely condescending – implying that my view of John and Jessie Frémont was goodhearted but suffered from excessive naiveté. That was his phrase, exactly."

"That's a peculiar detail," Jupiter said. "I'm glad you remember it so clearly. I understand that the producers hired Hernández for 'balance' after OUTLAW began protesting. But why him and not someone else entirely?"

"I have no idea" Dr. Paxton said.

Pete was so intent on the conversation that he jumped when the phone on a side table rang. Phillipa Paxton picked it up.

"Yes," she said. "This is Phillipa Paxton." She listened for a moment and then asked the person on the other end to hold. She turned to Pete and his friends, her eyes wide. "It's the Sonoma police," she said, "with information. I'm going to put the phone on speaker." She pressed a button. "Go ahead, officer," she said. "I wanted my colleagues to hear this."

Wow! Pete thought. Colleagues!

"As I was saying, Dr. Paxton," an authoritative female voice said. "The young man who attacked you has been very difficult to deal with, but we've discovered that his real name is Donovan Jones. Are you familiar with that name?"

Bob nudged Jupiter and whispered, "Any relation?" Jupiter smiled briefly, then went back to listening.

"No, officer," Dr. Paxton said. "That doesn't ring a bell."

"How about Dasan Coyote?" the officer asked. "That's what he actually calls himself."

"Excuse me?" Dr. Paxton said.

"I'm afraid the boy's deeply disturbed," the officer said. "He claims he's the reincarnation of a Pomo Indian from the 19th century whose land was taken away by the American government. And what's more, he believes he's a Pomo bear-doctor − some sort of Native American berserker, apparently − with the power and invulnerability of a grizzly bear."

"But he isn't really a Native American at all?" Dr. Paxton asked.

"Well, we haven't done a DNA test," said the officer, laughing slightly, "but I don't think so."

"And he's remaining in custody?" Phillipa Paxton asked.

"For the time being. Of course, he may

eventually get out on bail, but the bail's been set quite high," the officer said. "And from what we can tell, the other members of this protest group he was with may be nuisances, but we don't think they're dangerous.

"And one last thing," the officer said. "I believe you know Dr. Daniel Hernández?"

"Yes," Dr. Paxton said. "We've met."

"It turns out that Donovan Jones was briefly enrolled at the university where Hernández teaches," the officer said. "In fact he took a course from Dr. Hernández last fall. That's all I have for you, but we'll be in touch."

After she hung up, Dr. Paxton sat staring straight ahead. Pete knew just how she felt. He was stunned. A man who thought he was a grizzly bear!

"What's a berserker?" he asked.

"Berserkers were Viking warriors who fought so furiously and for so long people thought they were in a trance," Jupiter told him. "They supposedly drew their power from bears."

Phillipa Paxton shook her head. "I shudder to think what that young man was taught. Thank goodness Hernández doesn't teach the history of the French revolution."

Jupiter cleared his throat. "This is all

171

very disturbing," he said. "But at least Donovan Jones poses no danger to you at the moment. What might pose a danger is something else. I'm sorry to ask this," he added, "but have you noticed anything at all — anything unusual around your house?"

Phillipa Paxton looked alarmed. "Why?" she asked.

"We looked at OUTLAW's Facebook page the other day," Pete said. "You've been doxxed. Someone posted your home address."

"Oh, Lord," she said. "Maybe that explains the footprints."

"The footprints?" Jupiter asked.

"I was taking out the recycling this morning, and I noticed some footprints by the garage door. Normally the ground is so hard in the summer that nothing would show, but I'd had the sprinkler on and the ground was soft. I didn't know where they'd come from."

"We'd better take a look," Jupiter said.

Dr. Paxton led them through the kitchen to the garage. She opened the garage door from inside, and the light of a California noon spilled in.

"Right there," she said, pointing.

Pete hunkered down on the edge of the concrete pad and stared at several outlines of a shoe. Some of them were on top of one another, and it was hard to really make them out.

"A man's shoe," Jupiter said. He pointed to one print in particular. "See how here we have only the front of the shoe? It seems the man wearing it was on tiptoe, trying to peer in through the garage door windows."

"Just one person?" Dr. Paxton asked. "Or a group?"

"From what I can observe," Jupiter said. "Just one."

Pete looked carefully. Sure enough, though there were a considerable number of footprints, they all did seem alike.

"And whoever it was was simply checking things out, not trying to get in," Jupiter said.

"How can you tell that?" Pete asked.

"If you look," Jupiter said, "you'll see there are no footprints near the door handle."

"Well, that's a relief, at least," Dr. Paxton said.

"Nevertheless, you need to report this to the local police," Jupiter said. "Especially after what happened at your office. I suggest you call Chief Reynolds. Do you know him?"

"I don't think I've ever met him," said Dr. Paxton, "but I know his name. You sound as if *you* know him."

"We met him when he came to our first grade class to talk about bicycle safety, but some years later – after he became Chief of Police – we got to know him better when we helped him out with a couple of cases."

"In fact," Pete added, "at the end of one of them, Chief Reynolds made us Rocky Beach junior deputies!"

"Of course, that was quite informal," said Jupiter deprecatingly.

"Well, maybe," Pete said, "but he gave us cards to carry in our wallets, and not long ago he also gave us his private cellphone number."

Pete had always liked Chief Reynolds. When he and Bob and Jupiter had first met him, he'd been in his early forties – easy-going and comfortable in his uniform, long-limbed and rangy, with a shock of black hair. He'd been a baseball star in college until a bad slide into third had derailed his career. He walked with a slight limp but had had no problem getting a job as a policeman in the town he'd grown up in.

Some years later, after he became Chief of Police, he'd started a community outreach program. Right from the start he'd taken The

Three Investigators seriously, treating them more like adults than like children. Now, though his once-dark hair was beginning to gray, he still seemed young — mixing strength with kindness in a way Pete found inspiring.

"I really don't think I need to call him yet," Phillipa Paxton said. "But I will, if things get worse." She sighed plaintively. "I thought it was wonderful when Richard Black asked me to write a screenplay based on my book, but it doesn't seem wonderful now."

"Just be careful and keep your door locked," Jupiter said. "We're going to do everything we can to get to the bottom of what's going on."

"I'm really grateful," Dr. Paxton said. "Just talking to the three of you has made me feel a good deal better."

It was true. Pete could see that Dr. Paxton's cheeks were less red, and in general she seemed calmer and more composed.

"We'll let you know as soon as we learn anything new," Jupiter said.

All three of them shook Dr. Paxton's hand. As Bob and Jupiter made for their bikes, Pete said, "Just a minute, guys." By himself he went over to the door to the garage, stepping carefully so as not to disturb any of the footprints they'd seen earlier. He studied them for a minute, remembering what Jupe had said about whoever having made them being on tiptoe. A man's shoes, Jupe had said. Though Pete still had a way to go to be as good at deduction as Jupe was, the only man *he* could think those shoes might belong to was Daniel Hernández!

9

Suspicious Behavior

All the way back to the Salvage Yard, Jupiter was thinking hard. If he hadn't decided it was preferable to keep his hands on the handlebars, he would have been pinching his lower lip. Usually when he rode his bike in Rocky Beach, he enjoyed exercising his powers of perception, checking to see in what little ways things had changed since he had last ridden the streets. But today his gaze was directed inward.

Pete had taken off for the Animal Rescue Center directly from Phillipa Paxton's house, so he and Bob were alone as they biked back to the Salvage Yard. When they pulled in, it was early afternoon and the place was quiet. Neither Jupiter's aunt nor his uncle could be seen, and Jupiter surmised that Uncle Titus was having his afternoon "lie down." From the workshop where Leif and Magnus spent their days came the sound of a bandsaw. Mallory MacLeod was nowhere to be seen.

"I thought Mallory might be working today," Bob said, and Jupiter detected the disappointment in his friend's voice.

"There's always another day," he said. "You'll see her soon enough."

"Yes," Bob said. "Do you think she's doing well at the job?"

"I have no idea," Jupiter said mildly. "You'd have to ask my aunt."

His voice sounded a little peevish, even to himself. It wasn't that he didn't like Mallory. In fact, he found himself strangely drawn to the way she thought. She was serious about everything she did, and he respected that. But the more often she was around the Salvage Yard, the greater the chance that either Pete or Bob would invite her into Headquarters − and Jupiter had been very clear about the fact that he thought that was a bad idea.

Since they'd turned the old mobile home into their headquarters some years ago, it had belonged to him and Pete and Bob and no one else. In fact, except for one or two of the boys they'd met in the course of solving their earliest cases, and some bad guys who they had lured inside in order to catch them, he, Pete, and Bob were the only ones who'd ever been inside − and Jupiter thought that since they were The Three Investigators and this was Three Investigators Headquarters, it would be a good idea to keep it that way. At some point, he might see the matter differently, he supposed, but he didn't think so.

He and Bob made some tomato sandwiches in Jupiter's aunt's kitchen and carried them to Headquarters. It was dim inside, a relief from the glare of the California sun, and as they ate, Jupiter put his mind to work.

He was actually feeling quite excited. Ever since the explosion on the movie set and the subsequent burning of the flags by OUT-LAW, Jupiter had been convinced there truly was a case here, but only after their visit to Phillipa Paxton's house had he felt convinced that he could solve it.

Well, not him alone, of course. It had really been very smart of Pete to ask his father about what appeared to be a discrepancy between what Daniel Hernández had told The Three Investigators when they'd met him in Sonoma and what Mr. Crenshaw had told Daniel Hernández about them before they ever got there.

Also, it had been important that the police had looked so thoroughly into the background of the young man who had assaulted Dr. Paxton. Of course, the policewoman had concluded that Donovan Jones was mentally ill, but to Jupiter, the fact that he was Hernández's ex-student seemed consequential. When he and Bob had both finished their sandwiches, Jupiter cleared his throat.

"What did you make of the call from the Sonoma policewoman?" Jupiter asked.

"I wasn't exactly surprised that this guy Donovan Jones believed he was some sort of a berserker," Bob said. "What struck me most was that he'd been one of Dr. Hernández's students. In general, it's a bad idea to judge people by the company they keep, but in this case, the association raises questions."

"I agree," Jupiter said. "I was also struck by what Dr. Hernández said to Dr. Paxton about her book. That it suffered from excessive 'naiveté.' Now where have we heard that word before?"

"Yes," Bob said. "I thought the same thing. 'Naiveté' is a word one professor might well use in conversation with another, but how likely is it that a protest group is going to go around chanting it?"

"Exactly," Jupiter said. "It seems to me too much of a coincidence. Although I have no hard evidence for this yet, it wouldn't surprise me if Dr. Hernández actually wrote OUTLAW's chant for them. And then of course Dr. Hernández's offer to buy some of Dr. Paxton's papers preceded the break-in at her office."

Bob looked startled "You think Hernández actually – "

"It's too early to think anything," Jupiter said. "At the moment it's all conjecture. But it would be good if we could kick some ideas around."

Jupiter got out a piece of paper and sharpened a pencil.

"I'll just make a list of what we know as we go along," he said.

At the top of the page he wrote DANIEL HERNÁNDEZ, SUSPECT.

"First," he said, "we know from the information Pete gleaned from his father that Hernández lied to us. Also, a man who would presumably have better things to do spent a good deal of time online doing research on The Three Investigators. This, despite the fact that he didn't know us and wasn't thinking of engaging us in the solution of a mystery."

"So he's nosy," Bob said.

"Or paranoid," Jupiter said. "If he had something to hide, he might well be a bit wary of the sudden appearance of three detectives, even if he thought of them as almost children."

He made a note on the piece of paper and underlined *paranoid*, then made another note and underlined *naiveté*.

"Now, as for Dr. Paxton's refusal to sell Dr. Hernández her papers, this would seem to give him a motive to be behind the break-in of her office."

"But Dr. Hernández was in Sonoma, along with Dr. Paxton, when her office was broken into. Isn't that right?" Bob said.

Jupiter sighed. "It would appear so," he said. "But Dr. Paxton said she hadn't seen him at all the day we met them both on the set. Perhaps he drove down from Sonoma the night before, got into her office building first thing in the morning, and then, after ransacking it, drove as quickly as possible back to Sonoma. That day was a Sunday, remember; there would have been just a skeleton staff in the college buildings."

"That's right!" said Bob. "The day we drove up there *was* a Sunday!"

"Since I can't believe that a man as apparently clever as Daniel Hernández would have risked using an accomplice – especially one as crazy as Donovan Jones – I think we should proceed on the assumption that he himself broke into Dr. Paxton's office. The next question is Why?" Jupiter said.

Bob said, "He must have wanted something he thought was in her office – maybe something to do with Kit Carson. My mom is always talking about how competitive everything has become at colleges these days – how hard it is to get an academic job, and to keep it. Since both Dr. Paxton and Dr. Hernández teach not only history, but the same history – since they're both supposedly experts on John Frémont – he might have been looking for something to help his career."

"I agree that if he was responsible for the break-in, Dr. Hernández's motive would have been to try to steal something he had been unable to buy," said Jupiter. "What I meant was that I don't see how anything Dr. Paxton might have wouldn't already have been available to him, in some form. After all, they're supposedly working from the same historical record. And he's already published his book."

"Let's see if we can find out any more about him online," Bob said.

He booted up the firm's desktop computer and started doing research while Jupiter sat beside him in a wooden chair. When Bob discovered that Hernández had his own website, with pictures of himself and his book, Jupiter wasn't at all surprised.

It was remarkable how much you could discover about a person online these days, Jupiter thought – and, if you participated in social media, there were thousands of snapshots of individual moments in your life, moments when you may not have been thinking clearly, or were acting stupidly.

Almost everyone's life was now an open book, and although as an investigator, Jupiter was gratified at how quickly and eagerly most people rushed to fill the pages of that book, as a human being, he was mystified and appalled.

In no time at all, he and Bob had discovered where Hernández had gone to college and to graduate school. They found the name of the community college where he had begun his academic career and then his move to a part-time position at the university in Los Angeles where he currently taught.

After some searching, Bob was also able to find the original scholarly paper that had later been expanded into his successful book. That paper had received a good deal of attention, and after the book elaborating its ideas had been published, Hernández had been hired into a full-time position – apparently because the head of his department had been so impressed by his discovery of one particular letter from Kit Carson to John Frémont.

"Boy," Bob said. "That was a lucky find."

According to what they read, Hernández had had the good fortune to discover the previously unknown letter hidden in the pages of a book that had been printed in 1863 – a book that Hernández had discovered among many old and forgotten books in an antiquarian bookstore in San Francisco.

"Why would Frémont have stuck a letter from Kit Carson in a book?" Bob wondered.

"Maybe he was using it as a bookmark," Jupiter said.

The Internet sources said that at first Hernández had thought the letter must be a fake. Since Kit Carson was illiterate, the body of the letter had been written by someone else, of course, but since it seemed to have been signed by Carson himself, Hernández had had the signature authenticated by a handwriting expert – a forensic document examiner from Boston. Sure enough; Daniel Hernández had discovered a lost Carson letter.

As Jupiter read the information Bob was pulling up, he understood that in certain academic circles, the letter had been a bombshell; mentions of it had even reached the mainstream press. It appeared to lay to rest a controversy that had simmered since the middle of the 19th century. During the Bear Flag Revolt, when Frémont had occupied the mission at San Rafael, three unarmed Mexicans had landed by boat nearby and had been shot to death by men under Frémont's command. Had they acted on their own, or under Frémont's orders?

Afterwards, it was rumored that Kit Carson himself had shot and killed the men, and that Frémont had ordered him to do so. However – at least as far as Jupiter could make out – the claim that this had happened did not appear in the historical record until John Frémont was running for President of the United States. At that point – ten years after the event – two men had testified to Frémont's involvement in the killing of the Mexicans.

One of the accounts was by the son of one of the victims, while the other was by a man who made no secret of his hatred of Frémont. His enemies had used the accounts to claim that Frémont was a murderer and a liar.

Jupiter was fascinated to learn that political smear campaigns had existed long before the present day, and he asked Bob to look online for a facsimile of the letter Hernández had discovered. Bob couldn't find one, but he did

find a typed version, and they discovered that
the letter read:

To the attention of John Charles Frémont:
*You have asked for a report and here it is. Al-
though I had some questions about the propriety of leaving the two surviving female settlers in a settlement so
dominated by men, I accepted your suggestion that to
bring them with us would involve arduous toil.*

*After seeing them securely quartered, I engaged in
some mercantile pursuits and provided myself with
a suitable horse. In truth, I hit pay dirt by obtaining a
magnificent chestnut mare.*

*We were all well armed and mounted and set
out with the first light of morning. With pleasant
weather and no enemy to fear, we should have reached
our destination in a long day's ride. Instead, we encountered hostile Indians, and after killing three of them,
drove the others off. Some Mexicans we met were also
killed. I assumed you would not object, since when we
encountered Don José Berreyesa and the sons of Don
Francisco de Haro near the shores of San Rafael, you
told me we had no room for prisoners.*

*The one day stretched to two as a result of our
encounters, but we are now safely in the Fort.*
C Carson.

Though the letter Daniel Hernández had
found might at first glance seem fairly dry and

boring, Jupiter quickly saw that it actually seemed to provide proof positive that the accusations against Frémont had been correct – that the first Senator from California was indeed responsible for the murder of three unarmed men. Finding this letter signed by Kit Carson had been a career-making event for Hernández.

Jupiter and Bob were engrossed in reading article after article about the controversy when Aunt Mathilda's voice came over the Salvage Yard intercom.

"Jupiter, are you there?" his aunt asked.

"Yes," Jupiter said.

"You have a visitor from out of town," Aunt Mathilda told him. "Dr. Daniel Hernández."

Jupiter looked at Bob and wondered if his own expression mirrored that of his friend. Bob looked shocked, and his mouth had even fallen a little open. His eyes were wide, almost as if he'd been caught doing something he shouldn't have been doing.

"Why do you think he's here?" Bob asked.

"I have no idea," Jupiter said. "But I don't think he knows we're looking him up online. Let's go find out what he wants."

The two of them left through Easy Three and closed the door behind them. They found Daniel Hernández in the Salvage Yard's office, talking to Aunt Mathilda.

"There you are," she said. "Dr. Hernández was just telling me he met you up in Sonoma."

"That's right," Jupiter said. He shook Hernández's hand. "Hello," he said. "This is unexpected."

"Well, unexpected for you, perhaps, but I've been hoping ever since I met you that I might stop by the place you've made so famous," Hernández said.

"I hope they've made it famous!" Aunt Mathilda said. "That is a consummation devotedly to be wished. It was a pleasure to meet you, Dr. Hernández. Now, if you'll excuse me." She smiled and walked off toward Leif and Magnus's workshop.

"I dropped by," Daniel Hernández said, "so I could give you a copy of my book. As I promised."

"Actually," Bob said, "we expected you to mail it."

Hernández smiled broadly. "Of course. But I had to go to the warehouse the movie producers rented; it's very near here and since

I was in the neighborhood, I thought it would be a pleasure to see you again. Is Pete – ?"

"Pete's volunteering at the Animal Rescue Center this afternoon," Jupiter told him.

"Well, please give him my regards and tell him I was sorry to miss him," Hernández said. "I was also very sorry to hear that Dr. Paxton was injured in the melee in Sonoma. I heard that at least they arrested the malefactor."

Since the 'malefactor' was someone Dr. Hernández had taught for a whole semester, Jupiter thought it was worth seeing if he gave any sign of recognition at the name.

"Yes," Jupiter said. "A man named Donovan Jones. Do you know him?"

Dr. Hernández pondered for a moment and then said, "Not that I know of. But Jones is a common name. Just like Hernández!"

He smiled, then said "Without further ado – " and handed Jupiter his book. After seeing Dr. Paxton inscribe the copy she had given The Three Investigators, Jupiter instinctively opened to the first pages of this one, and, sure enough, Daniel Hernández had inscribed it.

"For Jupiter, Pete, and Bob," the inscription read, "new friends and new readers. With my admiration and best wishes. Daniel

Hernández."

Jupiter handed the book to Bob, who at first seemed unable to think of anything to say, but who eventually remarked, "You really do have unusual handwriting. Have you ever taken a course in calligraphy?"

Hernández looked almost sad, as though not taking calligraphy courses had been one of the signal tragedies of his life. Jupiter couldn't help but feel he was being less than sincere when he said, "Alas, no. Ever since I first learned to write, I've been very careful about my letters. That's all."

"Well, thank you very much for this book," Bob said. "I'm sure all three of us will do our best to get around to reading it."

Now it was Bob, Jupiter thought, who was being less than sincere.

"Yes," Jupiter added quickly. "And for taking the time to deliver it personally."

"You're very welcome," Daniel Hernández said. "I'll get a lot of pleasure out of thinking of the three of you turning my pages. Well, I must be off. By the way, do you boys have a new case?"

When Bob again looked at a loss, Jupiter said, "Nothing of any importance. We're looking for a man named John Lysander Smith.

You wouldn't know anyone by that name, would you?"

"Indeed, no," Hernández said. "But all good luck."

After he had gotten in his car and left, Jupiter and Bob went back into Headquarters. Jupiter felt a little shaken from their unexpected encounter with a man he had just identified on paper as DANIEL HERNÁNDEZ, SUSPECT, but if Hernández had thought that a visit to the Jones Salvage Yard would allay whatever suspicions The Three Investigators might have had, he was sorely mistaken.

"I have a hunch," Jupiter said aloud. "Let's do a search for 'Daniel Hernández' and 'calligraphy.'"

Bob typed the words in the Search box and hit Enter.

A stylish page popped right up: Handwriting By Hernández, Calligraphy For Every Occasion.

It turned out that when Daniel Hernández had been a part-time teacher, teaching by the course, and making very little money, he had supplemented his income by doing work as a calligrapher − creating sophisticated invitations, beautiful certificates, fancy calling cards and business cards, indeed anything that could be enhanced with highly artistic handwriting.

"No way!" said Bob. "He just lied to our faces!"

"He did, indeed," said Jupiter. "He was taken aback by your question, and in his haste to find an answer, he answered with a lie."

"But why?" said Bob.

"I have no idea," Jupiter admitted. "but I think it might be useful if we reviewed what we've got so far, by way of reasons to be suspicious of Daniel Hernández.

"In the first place, he did research on us before he met us, for no apparent reason – unless he was worried that we were coming to the set to investigate *him*. In addition, he used the word 'naiveté' when talking to Dr. Paxton and OUTLAW used the same word in their protest chant.

"He was absent from the set of *Bear Valley* at a time when Dr. Paxton's office was broken into – and he had previously tried to buy Dr. Paxton's Kit Carson letters. In addition, he claimed never to have taken a calligraphy course, when he once made a living with calligraphy. Finally, an ex-student of his, who he claimed not to know, and who more or less attacked Dr. Paxton in Sonoma, was arrested with a garrote in his pocket, and Hernández himself was in the proximity of the keg of gunpowder when someone lit the fuse."

"The last two may be true," Bob said. "But what would Hernández gain from hurting Dr. Paxton or blowing up the set?"

Jupiter shook his head.

"I don't know," he said. "Suspicions are merely that – we have no hard evidence. No smoking gun, as they say. It's all just circumstantial.

"However, the most annoying thing about this list is that, although Hernández may be in cahoots with OUTLAW and may also be responsible for the break-in, I can't see how the two connect. I also can't see where Hernández's lie about calligraphy comes in. It's not as if Daniel Hernández was a forger or something."

He pinched his lower lip.

"Am I missing something, Bob?"

"Not that I can think of," Bob said.

"I'll keep thinking about it," Jupiter said. "Depend on that. And don't forget; I have every reason to expect that tonight you'll find information that leads us to John Lysander Smith. You'd better get going, or you're going to be late for dinner."

10

An Ingenious Plan

As it happened, Bob *was* late for dinner, but only by a little, and since his father was cooking that night, it didn't really matter. His father was easy-going about just about everything except his work as a journalist for the Los Angeles *Sun*. He was a tall man, with reddish-blond hair parted on the side, and a sly ironic sense of humor. He liked to poke fun at Bob occasionally, but he always made it clear how proud of him he was.

Bob's mother was different. Maxine Andrews seemed very young – almost girlish – but as an evolutionary biologist, she was both practical and logical, and although she looked almost classically Chinese, she had a gentle, pitying sort of smile with which she seemed to contemplate the foibles of humanity. She had met Bob's father when he was doing an article on recent Chinese immigration to the United States, and they had been happily married ever since. They agreed on all the big, important things, but disagreed about some of the small ones.

In fact, if *she* had been cooking tonight, Bob thought, his mother would have asked him why he was late – and he would have been happy to tell her! Since he wanted to tell her, anyway, Bob had just sat down to dinner when he began talking. He had already filled his parents in on what had happened in Sonoma, but he wanted to give them an update about the latest.

"I told you about that protest group, OUTLAW, that we saw up in Sonoma?" Bob said. "Today Dr. Paxton told us they're trying to get students from all over to join. Including at Reedmore." He turned to his mother only to see her faintly pitying smile.

"Yes," she said. "They're everywhere now."

"I didn't know you knew about them," Bob said.

"Their portfolio seems to extend beyond what they call lawbreakers," she said. "They've taken to objecting to scientific facts about genetics and evolution. Like the fact that both the human species and individual human beings are born with certain predispositions. They want to believe that people are born as blank slates."

"Wow," Bob said. "I had no idea."

"Teaching used to be about the transmission of knowledge, but it's become totally politicized," his mother added.

"That's true where I work, too," Mr. Andrews said. "News reporting at least used to *try* to be objective, but now every article reads as though it belongs on the Opinions page. We journalists need to work as hard as we can to present facts, not opinions – to stick to the objective truth."

"Anything else is basically propaganda," his mother agreed. "You wouldn't think people would fall for propaganda as quickly and easily as they do. Science never puts a political agenda ahead of a willingness to follow evidence wherever it leads. Science investigates everything – just the way The Three Investigators do. What else did Dr. Paxton tell you?"

"While we were up in Sonoma, somebody broke into her office at the college, and Jupiter thinks it may have been the other historian working on *Bear Valley* – a guy named Daniel Hernández."

"Why would Daniel Hernández want to break into Dr. Paxton's office?" asked his father.

"He might have been looking for some letters written by Kit Carson. Hernández tried to buy them from Dr. Paxton, but she wasn't interested in selling," Bob explained. "Dr. Paxton thinks that OUTLAW was behind the break-in, though — that they were trying to cause her problems. To scare her, really."

Bob's father looked thoughtful. "As a reporter, I've discovered that when people break into other people's spaces, they almost always want to steal something," he said. "Though they're happy if other people get the blame."

"As an evolutionary biologist, I would agree with that," his mother said. "I hope the trouble is over now."

Although Bob supposed that he should hope that, too, he actually didn't. He hoped the case developed and came to a logical conclusion. However, right now, he had other things to think about, and when dinner was over, Bob helped his father with the dishes, then went to his room to see if he could locate anyone named John Lysander Smith.

The name Lysander had a long history, Bob discovered. It was the name of a Spartan general in ancient Greece, and the name of a main character in Shakespeare's play "A Midsummer Night's Dream." In more contemporary times, it was most well known as the first name of Lysander Spooner. Spooner had been a 19th-century attorney, abolitionist, and anarchist philosopher who wrote a book on the unconstitutionality of slavery. For a moment, Bob wondered whether Spooner could have known John Frémont. After all, they had lived at basically the same time, and they were both well-known abolitionists.

Interesting as that idea might be, Bob needed to get serious about what he was doing, and he started to look up *Lysander* in combination with other words. He typed "John Lysander Smith" and "collector" into the search bar and came up with sites selling collectible books by Lysander Spooner. "Lysander" and "Sonoma" led to a star athlete from Sonoma State. "Lysander" and "quilt" led to a line of bedding.

Bob finally found a John Lysander Smith on a Fiftieth Reunion class list for Claremont McKenna College in Claremont, California – not all that far from Rocky Beach. According to the college records, this particular Smith had attended the reunion just the year before and would be in his early seventies. There was no address or phone number, but Bob assumed that if he called the college the next day, someone in the Alumni Office would have that information. Before he went to bed, he called Jupiter on the landline.

"I found him!" he said. "Or rather I found a John Lysander Smith who graduated from Claremont McKenna College fifty years ago. I still don't know if he's the one who lived in Sonoma, but how many men with that name, and the right approximate age, could there be?"

"I agree," Jupiter said. "Good work, Bob."

"You don't sound as excited as I thought you'd be," Bob said, a bit deflated.

"I'm frustrated," Jupiter said. "All evening I've been thinking about Daniel Hernández. There's something I'm missing, but I can't quite think of what it could be. I mean, I feel we already have an important clue, but it's not in the right place telling us the right thing. So I stopped trying to puzzle it through and started reading *Bear Valley*. It's quite interesting."

"I know what you mean about the clue," Bob said. "I was telling my father about the break-in at Dr. Paxton's office, and he said something I keep thinking about – though I'm not exactly sure why. Anyway, in the morning I'll call the college and if I can get the information about this John Lysander Smith, I'll come over to the Salvage Yard. I think it would be best if all three of us were together when we called. Otherwise he might think I was some crank. We can urge him to look us up online, if he wants, and if we call from our official phone he's more likely to take us seriously. Would you call Pete and set it up?"

"Sure," Jupiter said. "Good night."

The next morning Bob called the Alumni Office at Claremont McKenna College. The woman he spoke to was very kind, but sorry to tell him that she couldn't release personal information about alumni to non-alumni. But she gave Bob a lead. She suggested he search the Claremont McKenna alumni magazine for the class coordinator for the class of 1972. Perhaps he'd be willing to share the information with Bob.

Bob quickly found what he was looking for. The man's name was Alex Sanders, and both his telephone number and e-mail address were listed. He biked to the Salvage Yard as quickly as he could. There, he saw Mallory MacLeod entering the office, and he waved to her as he went to find Pete and Jupiter. When Bob joined them in the outdoor workshop, Pete said, "Jupiter's figured something out!"

"What is it?" Bob asked.

"He wants us to call about the flag quilt

first."

"Everything in its place," Jupiter agreed. "Let's finish one thing before we start another."

They piled into Headquarters through Easy Three and got settled around the desk in their customary chairs. Bob punched Alex Sanders's phone number and hit the button for Speaker. The phone was picked up on the third ring.

"Hello?" a hearty male voice said.

"Is this Mr. Alexander Sanders?" Bob asked.

"Yes," Mr. Sanders said. "And who is this, please?"

"My name is Bob Andrews, Mr. Sanders, and I was directed to your number by the Claremont McKenna Alumni Office. I think you were the coordinator for last year's fiftieth reunion."

"That's correct," Mr. Sanders said, his voice cautious.

Bob explained why he was calling and introduced Jupiter and Pete. When Bob hesitantly mentioned the Isabella Chang case and the discovery of the gold, Mr. Sanders's voice changed.

"Why yes," he said. "I remember reading in the paper about you boys. So you're looking for Lyle Smith? That's his nickname, of course. Lyle and I were very good friends when we were undergraduates. He lives in Los Angeles now. Let me go get his information for you."

Bob heard the sound of a receiver being put down and all was quiet for a while. He looked at Jupiter and Pete. Pete was grinning and Jupiter looked quite pleased.

"Hello, Bob?" Mr. Sanders said. "I'm back." He gave Bob the information, and then repeated it so there would be no misunderstanding. "And give him my regards!" Mr. Sanders added. "Tell him I said he and I should have lunch!"

"I will," Bob said. "Thank you very much." Bob hung up the phone and took a deep breath.

"Well," Jupiter said. "Very close now. Let's not dawdle."

Bob dialed Lyle Smith's number and looked at his friends expectantly. Through the speaker they heard the phone ring, again and again, and Bob was about to hang up, disappointed, when the phone was picked up.

The man's voice was softer and gentler than his friend Alex Sanders's had been. "Lyle Smith," he said politely.

"Mr. Smith?" Bob said. "My name is Bob Andrews, and I'm calling because I think you may once have lived in an Arts and Crafts house in Sonoma. I'm on a speaker phone with my friends Jupiter Jones and Pete Crenshaw, and we've been hired to try to track you down, to ask you something. The name of our firm is The Three Investigators, if you want to look us up before you talk."

"My goodness," said Lyle Smith. "Ask me what?"

"So you did live in Sonoma, in an Arts and Crafts house?" Jupiter asked, taking over the conversation. "This is Jupiter Jones speaking."

"I did indeed, young man. At least, from your voice, I'm guessing that you're young. I moved to Los Angeles in 1998. Why do you want to know?"

"Our friend Branko Petrovic lives in your old house now, and he found some invoices and other papers with your name on them. We represent a collector who is interested in a flag you used to own. Well, really, it's a flag quilt — a replica of a commemorative flag that Jessie Frémont had made for her husband. The collector's name is Phillipa Paxton," Jupiter said.

"Now, that's very interesting," Lyle

Smith said. "You're the second person who's asked me about that quilt in the last two weeks. The other man told me he was a professor at a university in L.A., but when I said I wasn't interested in selling, he thanked me and hung up. I haven't heard from him again."

"What was his name?" Jupiter asked tensely.

"I don't think he ever told me," Lyle Smith said.

"I see," said Jupiter. "Well, Dr. Paxton will be disappointed that you don't want to sell the quilt, but I'm glad to know at least you still have it. Would it be possible for us to come and see it, and talk to you?" he added.

"I'm free tomorrow," Lyle Smith said. "Come by at 11:00 if you like."

"We will," said Jupiter. "Thank you very much. See you then." He hung up the phone and turned to Bob and Pete who had both started talking at once.

"That professor *must* have been Daniel Hernández!" Pete exclaimed, while Bob said, at almost the same instant, "How did Dr. Hernández track down Lyle Smith?"

Jupiter looked at them gravely. "Remember that Dr. Paxton told us that Hernández offered to trade or barter as well as buy, and since we know he's good at eaves-dropping, I imagine he overheard Phillipa Paxton talking about this quilt she wanted and thought he'd see if he could get a hold of it before she did."

"How did he track it down, though?" Bob asked again.

"He could have contacted the Sonoma paper and asked them to put him in touch with the original writer of the article. If the Ghost-to-Ghost hookup hadn't worked, that was what I planned to do myself."

"Of course!" said Bob. "Whenever my father writes an article for the paper, he saves his notes for future reference. And you know, speaking of my father, I've been thinking about something he said to me last night at dinner. He said that, as a reporter, he's discovered that people who break and enter almost always want to steal something, but they're happy if other people get the blame. Is it possible that Daniel Hernández has just been *using* this OUT-LAW group? Getting them all riled up about Phillipa Paxton and her book so that the police will blame them for the break-in at her office?"

"Excellent thinking, Records," Jupiter said. "I had formed the same tentative hy-pothesis myself. Unfortunately, we need more evidence before we can call it a conclusion."

"So tell us what you discovered!" Pete said.

Bob could see that Jupiter was both excited by what he'd found and also proud of himself. He lifted the copy of *Bear Valley* from the desk and opened it.

"I looked up Kit Carson in the index of Dr. Paxton's book to see if she'd written about any of the letters she showed us yesterday. Sure enough, right here – " he stabbed the open book with his finger – "there's a rather lengthy passage about one of the letters we saw. And then I realized that since Hernández also read *Bear Valley*, he'd have read the same passage.

"As you and I found out, Bob, the whole reason Hernández went from being a part-time teacher to being a regular professor was because of a Kit Carson letter he'd discovered." He sat back and crossed his arms on his chest.

"And?" Pete said. "Come on, Jupe. Out with it."

"And," Jupiter said, "I discovered that both the bombshell letter that made Hernández's career and the letter we saw yesterday were written on the exact same day!"

He paused for effect. Sometimes Jupiter's training as a child actor served him well,

Bob thought.

"But the letters are about totally different things," Jupiter added. "Hernández's letter is a report which details an encounter with hostile Indians and Mexicans, while Dr. Paxton's letter is about advice Carson is giving Frémont about terrain to the north of where Frémont is stationed. I wish I'd been able to see the original of Hernández's letter so that I could see if the handwriting on the letters matched. If they don't, it would seem almost certain that – "

"That one of the letters is a fake!" Pete yelled.

"What are the odds that two different people would have written two different letters to John Frémont, both for Carson's signature, from two different places on the same day?" Bob agreed.

"Although Hernández had a document expert attest to Carson's signature, and, as far as we know, Dr. Paxton hasn't," Jupiter said, "I think we must now all share the suspicion as to which letter is the forgery."

"So what do we do next?" Pete asked.

"I wish there were some way I could talk to Hernández again without alerting him to our suspicions," Jupiter said. "You know the way he told us how much he liked to talk to young people about history? It's too bad he knows us, or else one of us could make an appointment to see him in his office. I'd tell him what a fan I'd always been of Kit Carson and how disappointed I'd been to hear that he and John Frémont were cold-blooded murderers."

Jupiter stared off at the wall as if he were imagining himself in Hernández's office.

"I'd say how fascinating it would be to see the actual letter. I'd tell him I hadn't been able to find it online, that, in fact, I had the feeling it had never been made public. And he had to have a scan of it on his computer, didn't he? Could I see it? I'd say. If I could, I'd at least know whether or not the handwriting of the letter was the same or different from the handwriting in Dr. Paxton's."

"I could go," Bob said. "He suggested it himself when he gave us his card."

"It's too risky," Jupiter said. "He may already suspect we're onto him, and the minute you brought up Kit Carson, he'd know why you were there. He may be a liar, but he's very clever."

"Well, I saw Mallory MacLeod when I got here. Maybe she could do it," Bob said. "She loved helping us on the last case, and you know how smart she is. She can think on her feet, and I'm sure she'd understand in no time what we were hoping she could do. Why don't we ask her, Jupe?"

Jupiter pinched his lower lip. Bob could see he was wrestling with himself. Part of him didn't want to involve Mallory in this, but a bigger part wanted to solve the mystery.

"That's a very good idea, Bob," he said. "If she agrees, she could call Hernández and ask to meet him in his office. Better if she tells him right away she's interested in Carson. It's a bit tricky that she has a Scottish accent."

"Why can't a Scot be interested in Carson?" Pete asked. "She might even be able to turn it to her advantage."

"True enough," Jupiter said, getting to his feet. "We're agreed. Let's go find her. You ask her, Bob."

They found her cataloging old lamp fixtures behind one of the sheds. She seemed pleased to see them, Bob thought.

"We wanted to ask a favor, Mallory," he said. "We need help with our current case. Are you willing to go undercover?"

Bob explained the situation as quickly as he could.

"So, for now, I'm just calling this professor and asking to come in and speak with him in his office?" Mallory asked.

"Correct," Jupiter said.

"How do I know about him in the first place?"

"You could say you heard about him from your mother, who's working on the movie," Bob said, "and that your mother has a copy of his book."

"But I can't let him know that I know you," she said.

"Correct again," Jupiter said. "You've never met us – never even heard of us."

"And you want me to get a copy of the letter if I can – so that you can compare Carson's supposed secretary's handwriting with the handwriting on Phillipa Paxton's Carson letter."

"Yes," Bob said. "We're going in to L.A. tomorrow, anyway – to visit a man who owns the original replica of the Frémont flag your mother's been making – so you could come with us to visit him, and then we could go on to Daniel Hernández's office. Why don't you meet us here at 10:00 and try to make an appointment with Dr. Hernández for 1:00 or something?"

"That should work," Mallory said. "How are we going to get there?"

Bob and Pete and Jupiter all looked at one another with dismay.

"If we had our car, Worthington could drive us," Pete said.

"Not necessarily. Remember, Worthington is working for himself now, and he won't be able to drop what he's doing at a moment's notice," Jupiter said.

"Maybe Leif or Magnus could drive us," Bob suggested. "Like Hans and Konrad used to do sometimes."

"If Uncle Titus says it's O.K., that would work," Jupiter said. "He's in charge of the trucks."

The four of them walked into Leif and Magnus's workshop. The brothers were wearing safety goggles and working with power tools, and when they saw who had entered, they quickly turned the tools off and hurried to the door.

"Wait, wait," Magnus said. "That's far enough."

Bob suddenly understood that they had probably been working on the immigrant's chest, and he quickly suggested they all step outside.

"Yes, yes," Magnus said, shoving Leif. "You go. I stay here." He looked vastly relieved.

Bob and the others retreated to the outside.

Mallory looked at Leif strangely. "Why do you always seem so nervous when I show up?" she asked.

"No, no," Leif said, exploding with nervous laughter. "We like you! We just don't like to be surprised."

"I'll say," Mallory said.

"Anyway," Jupiter said. "We were wondering if it might be possible for you or Magnus to drive the four of us into L.A. tomorrow. We don't know how else to get there."

"I could maybe take you tomorrow morning," Leif said. "I first have to check with Mr. Jones, of course."

"Of course," Jupiter said. "We have an appointment at 11:00."

"So we will meet here at 10:00," Leif said. "I'm sure Titus will agree. That man is a good boss."

"But Mrs. Jones is the real boss," Pete said.

"That, too," Leif said.

So it was agreed. They'd meet tomorrow morning at the Salvage Yard at 10:00. Leif shook hands all around, unnecessarily, and then, laughing to himself, went back into the workshop.

"They must have odd customs in Norway," Mallory observed. "Well, I'd better get going. I want to do some research on Carson so I don't look like a total muppet." Bob took Daniel Hernández's card from his backpack so he could give Mallory the number. She carefully wrote it down. "Well, then," she said. "See you tomorrow at ten."

As Mallory took off on her bike, Bob smiled. "So?" he asked Jupe.

Jupiter nodded. "I have the sense she'll be very good," he said. "Maybe better than any of us could have been. I think she'll fool him completely."

"Me too," Bob said. "She'll be terrific." He was very glad he'd thought of the idea.

11

An Amazing Find

The next morning, Pete sat at the kitchen table with a bowl of cereal while his mother washed dishes. She soaped them and rinsed them and held each one up for inspection as if the future of the world depended on her getting it perfectly clean. She was almost as intense about washing dishes as she was about her Tarot cards and the I Ching and her willow hoop Ojibwe dreamcatcher. Boy, Pete thought, she was intense.

But she was also loads of fun. Her laughter was an explosion of happiness. Today she was wearing hoop earrings partially hidden by the curly black hair that cascaded over her shoulders. She had strong emotions, which she constantly expressed. To Pete, she seemed the opposite of his father. While Martín was generally pretty laid-back – though not about Daniel Hernández! – Valeria was high-strung, but the two of them balanced one another nicely, Pete thought.

His mother examined the last dish, then came and sat at the table with him. "I have the feeling you want to ask me a question," she said.

Pete looked at her, surprised. "How did you know?" he asked.

She smiled. "After all," she said, "I *am* your mother."

Pete picked up his cereal bowl and drank the last bit of milk. "So," he said, "it's about reincarnation. Which you believe in, right?"

"Absolutely," his mother said. "As I've told you, I'm almost certain you're the reincarnated spirit of one of the Niños Héroes from the Battle of Chapultepec."

According to his mother, Pete had previously died during the Mexican-American War. Maybe that was why he knew so little about it.

"Anyway," Pete said. "There's this guy who was arrested on the set of Dad's movie up in Sonoma. His name is Donovan Jones but he says that he's the reincarnation of a Pomo Indian bear-doctor."

"Good for him," his mother said. "Most people are unaware of their previous incarnations."

"But the police think he's crazy," Pete said.

"Yes, of course," his mother said. "Many people still think reincarnation is crazy.

But it's not. Not usually, anyway."

Outside, a horn sounded. Pete jumped up and kissed his mother on the cheek. "Got to go," he said.

Pete ran to the curb where one of the Salvage Yard's trucks waited – a Ram 2500, with a big backseat. Though they'd planned on meeting at the Salvage Yard, Jupiter had called that morning to say they'd pick Pete up instead. Mallory was riding shotgun. Pete joined Jupe and Bob in the back and said hello to everyone.

"I was just talking to my mother about this Dasan Coyote and reincarnation," he said.

Jupiter looked at Pete with mild apprehension. "Your mother is terrific," he said, "but you know I don't believe in her superstitions."

"Neither do I!" Pete said. "Most of the time. But Dasan Coyote believed it. He yelled 'I wear the skin of the grizzly bear' when everyone could see he was wearing shorts and a t-shirt. What *is* a bear-doctor, anyway?"

"I did some research on that," Bob said. "The Pomo believed these 'bear-doctors' were imbued with special powers of fierceness and invulnerability when they dressed in bearskins. A lot of the tribes of central California believed that some of their members were given special powers by grizzly bears and could actually transform themselves into grizzlies."

"This is when there still *were* grizzlies in California," Pete said.

Bob nodded. "The Pomo bear-doctors just wore skins, and the Pomo believed that they had the right to kill four people a year with total impunity. They also had helpers – assistants they would pass their knowledge on to. That was how the practice continued."

"What does impunity mean?" Pete asked.

"They weren't punished for killing other people, as long as they stuck to only four a year," Bob explained.

"That's a pretty weird belief," Pete said.

"It helps explain why this guy who calls himself Dasan Coyote was carrying a garrote in his backpack," Bob said.

Mallory hadn't heard this part of the story yet, so when she asked, Pete and Bob and Jupiter filled her in on everything they knew.

"This guy sounds pretty dangerous," she said.

"At the moment, he's still in jail," Jupiter said. "So even if he truly believes he's been granted the right to kill people, he won't be able to do it. Still, I'm intrigued by what Bob

218

discovered. The Sonoma policewoman called Pomo bear-doctors berserkers, but berserkers were actually Viking warriors who believed they became bears in the heat of battle."

"Yes," Leif chimed in suddenly. "When I was growing up in Norway, I learned that in a battle they would howl and bite their shields."

Leif took his hands off the steering wheel and made claws of them, then growled and pawed at the air in front of him.

They all started laughing, but Pete kept thinking about just how dangerous this guy Donovan Jones might really be. He was glad the bail had been set so high that he wouldn't be getting out of jail anytime soon.

John Lysander Smith's house was not hard to find. It was in Sherman Oaks, one of the northern sections of the great sprawl that is Los Angeles. As they got closer and closer, Pete realized again how lucky he was to live in Rocky Beach. Here the freeway had five lanes in each direction and the houses were packed one next to the other. But Smith lived on a relatively quiet street, and when they pulled up in front of it, Pete could immediately see that Mr. Smith was a rich man.

The house was very modern, a long rectangular glassy box. The front yard had a small grassy area with an old palm tree, but the rest was a sculpture garden, with the sculptures resting on a finely raked pebble bed.

Steel girders and posts framed the building, enclosing large expanses of sheet glass, occasionally interrupted by narrow vertical sections of dull gray wood. Pete thought it could get hot inside that house very quickly.

Mallory, Jupiter, Bob, and Pete climbed out of the truck. "Take your time," Leif said. "I'll be right here."

As they walked down the pebble walk, Pete was surprised to see that the drapes had not been drawn and they could peer right into the living room, where a man wearing what looked like black pajamas was standing on his head. His elbows were propped on the floor and he looked completely still.

As they watched, he lowered his legs slowly until his toes touched the floor, and then he crouched over his knees with his head bent in front of him. Was this the right house?

Jupiter rang the doorbell and in less than a minute the man in the black pajamas answered the door. Pete could see now that it was a martial arts outfit of some kind, belted at the waist and made of thin cotton. The man had what Pete recognized as an Egyptian ankh on

a silver chain around his neck, and several tur-
quoise rings on his fingers. His face was very
red and surprisingly youthful for someone in his
early 70s. He had a full head of white hair, a
bit mussed from the upside-down-ness, and an
expectant smile on his face.

"You caught me!" he said. "You must be
The Three Investigators, and – ?" He looked
expectantly at Mallory.

"I'm Mallory MacLeod," she said. "A
friend of theirs."

"Come in, come in," the man said. "I'm
Lyle Smith, but my friends call me Lysander.
Ha ha, only kidding. But I do admire my
namesake, Lysander Spooner. In *Trial by Jury*,
he defended the doctrine of jury nullification."

Pete had no idea what that was, and although he knew that the best way of getting an
answer to a question was to ask it, in this case,
he didn't want to.

Luckily, Jupiter said, "An important
American legal doctrine – though not as widely
known today as it should be."

Mr. Smith looked at Jupiter with interest,
then led the way into the foyer.

"The four of you look quite fit," he said.
"How do you do it? I mainly do Tai Chi and
yoga now, but I used to be quite a swimmer."

"Bicycling mostly, I guess," Pete said. "I play soccer in school."

"Good for you, good for all of you. A healthy life is a life well-lived, and you've got to keep active if you want to live a healthy life. Alas, Cornelius has not kept active – Cornelius Patterson, my partner – and thus he is not here right now to greet you. Actually, he's in the hospital with a slipped disc."

"Ouch," Pete said. "I bet that's painful."

"So he says," Mr. Smith said. "Quite frequently. He's an art restorer by profession – the best in the business if I do say so myself. But he spends too much time in dim rooms, hunched over old paintings. He needs to straighten up, breathe deeply, let the ch'i flow."

"The what?" Pete asked.

"The life force." Lyle Smith threw his shoulders back, made circles with his thumbs and forefingers, stood as tall as he could, and took a deep breath. "You should try it," he said.

Maybe, Pete thought. But not right now.

"Anyway," Lyle continued. "I run the household and Cornelius keeps me sane. When he's not around, I get a bit muddled, really."

"Maybe you just need some company,"

Mallory said. "Couldn't you hire someone to come and help for a while?"

"Yes, of course," Mr. Smith said. "But having strangers around can be so annoying, don't you think? Even if they only come part time. Most of them are so boring. And pushy. I don't know if I could bear it."

"We just met someone I think you'd like," Pete said. "If you don't mind my saying so, you seem a bit – um – unusual – "

"Pete!" Bob said.

"And *she* is certainly unusual," Pete said. "Her name is Charlotte Mitchell and she works part-time for our friend Isabella Chang. She's a really good cook and very friendly. And she dresses like a fortune teller."

"Hmm," Mr. Smith said. "Is she smart?"

"Isabella Chang seems to think so," Jupiter said. "And Ms. Chang is certainly smart."

"That sounds good," Mr. Smith said. "Perhaps I'll give the young woman a telephone call. Is she young?"

"In her thirties, I think," Bob said.

"Not so young then," Mr. Smith said. "Better and better. But you didn't come here to address my domestic arrangements, did you? You're here about the Frémont quilt. As I said, that beautiful piece has resided quietly in this house for many years – not a peep out of it or about it – and suddenly, within two weeks, I've had two phone calls. What are the odds?"

"I can explain that, I think," Jupiter said. "We represent Dr. Phillipa Paxton, who collects Frémont memorabilia, and it seems likely that the man who contacted you wanted to use the quilt as a means of barter with Dr. Paxton."

"Hmm," Mr. Smith said. "Interesting. But I'm forgetting myself. I should already have offered you something to drink. Come with me to the kitchen."

Inside, the house seemed very large and was flooded with light. Several marble pedestals stood at intervals and on each was a crystal vase filled with flowers – lilies in one, gladioli in another. Several held lush arrangements of orchids in ceramic pots. The walls were covered with frames: framed art and posters and other things Pete didn't recognize. On small metal and glass tables was an assortment of beautiful handmade baskets.

Pete paused before a section of wall covered with framed photographs. In almost all of them, two men stared back at him. One of the men was Lyle Smith. The other was a thin handsome man with cinnamon-brown skin and short bouncy dreadlocks. He was a little bit taller than Lyle. In one he was wearing a tuxedo; in another a caftan; in a third, jeans and a sweatshirt. No matter what he was wearing, he managed to look elegant. He had a dazzling smile.

"Now you've met Cornelius," Lyle said, "or as close as you'll get until they release him from his bed of pain. He comprises worlds. He's part Samoan, part African-American, part Najavo, and part English."

"Wow!" Pete said. He couldn't wait to meet him.

In the kitchen, he stared at the enormous shiny brushed-metal appliances – a big stove with a hood, an industrial-sized refrigerator, and a gleaming double sink. Mr. Smith opened the refrigerator.

"I can offer you a variety of sparkling waters," he said. "Grapefruit, pomegranate, Asian pear?"

Pete was tempted to say he wasn't thirsty, but he was, so he chose the grapefruit and found he liked it. The five of them carried their drinks back to the living room where Pete, Jupiter, Bob, and Mallory all sat on the single enormous sofa while Mr. Smith took up a cross-legged position on the floor.

"Can't be too comfortable," he said. "It's bad for you. At least as you get older. I never thought I'd get this old, but here I still am. And still collecting. The Frémont quilt is in a box in the storage room – along with a lot of other things. I have artifacts from eight or nine native California tribes as well as documents, fabrics, and artworks from the Mexican settlers who came to California and the Americans who came after them. I also have work by early California artists like Alfred Bierstadt and George Inness. I'm a bit old-fashioned in my tastes," he added.

"What are you going to do with all this stuff?" Pete asked curiously. "Eventually, I mean," he said, but then said, "Sorry," when Jupiter and Bob shot him reproving glances.

Still, right now what Pete was actually regretting was that, not all that long ago, he had imagined that Dr. Paxton's desire to track down the commemorative flag quilt must be really pretty stupid. It seemed that he'd been wrong.

"There's no need to apologize, young man," said Mr. Smith. "All good things must come to an end. I intend to give my collection to museums. I should have done that long ago, but I have a hard time letting go of beautiful things. When I was an avid collector, I traveled to galleries and searched for things I heard about via word of mouth. In those days, I was also a museum curator. If you're done with your drinks, let's go get the Frémont quilt. We can look at it better in here."

He led the way down a narrow hallway to a large room at the back of the house. "When my collection got out of control," Mr. Smith said, "I had this storage room built at the back. Extravagant, really."

Pete saw that the room was filled with fully-laden shelves and piles of boxes. He watched as Mr. Smith opened a chest lined with redwood, and the sweet fragrance of the wood drifted out. Inside was a large box that Mr. Smith tried to lift but couldn't.

"Would you help me, young man?" he said to Pete. "Something this big weighs quite a lot."

Pete was surprised at how heavy it was. But then again, something that was twenty feet long by fifteen feet high was very large. Together, he and Mr. Smith carried the box down the hall and back to the living room where Mr. Smith took off the lid, removed the quilt, and began unfolding it. By the time he was done, it covered most of the room and was draped over the couch and several tables.

"You can see why I don't have this on display," Mr. Smith said. "I don't know who – other than a museum – would have a wall this big. My, it's beautiful. It's been so long since I looked at it."

As the flag quilt became visible, Pete was astonished at its size and its colors and its details. The original Bear Flag symbols were there – the star and the bear – but they were elaborately embroidered, and Pete thought he could see glimpses of landscape in the embroidery work.

"Look here," Mr. Smith said. He showed them the bottom of the quilt where, across the entire length, were sixteen embroidered flowers, each in its own block, with its Latin name. Each name contained a variation of Frémont. Mr. Smith explained that all of these flowers had either been named by, or named after, John Frémont.

Pete was fascinated by the quilt. Normally he paid little attention to things made of cloth. But when he looked closely, he was amazed at the delicacy and precision of the stitches.

"I can't believe someone did this with her

own hands," he said. "Look at how tiny all this work is. I bet every sewn thing I've ever seen was done by machine. I mean, I've never thought of sewing by hand as something that people actually *did*."

"Hand sewing is over twenty thousand years old," Mallory said, smiling. "Our ancestors made the first needles from animal bone or horn and the first thread from animal sinew."

Everyone went back to looking closely at the quilt. The top was like the Bear Flag, but on the bottom was a scene of Jessie and John and their daughter riding into the hills of their ranch in the Sierras. They were passing a grizzly bear with two cubs hiding behind a large pine tree – something that had really happened, Lyle explained.

"This is amazingly detailed," Bob said, "for something made in 1912 that's just a rendering of something else."

"Why do you say that?" Mallory asked.

"The 1860 flag quilt that Jessie Frémont had made for her husband burned up in the fires after the San Francisco earthquake," Mr. Smith said. "This one was made by someone who reproduced it based on photographs."

Mallory looked skeptical. "I really don't think it was. This looks to me like something made in 1860, not in 1912. I think it's the original, not a copy."

There was total silence in the room.

"Really?" Pete exclaimed. "But how can you know that?"

"It's a lot of things," said Mallory. "The feel of the fabric, the fineness of the threads, the method of sewing. And look here."

She was staring at the hat on Jessie Frémont's head in the tableau at the bottom, Jessie and John on horseback. She pointed with her finger.

When Pete looked very closely, he could barely see what seemed to be two initials sewn into the hat band – the initials of the celebrated French seamstress who had made the original quilt for Jessie Frémont.

Pete felt a tingle start in his toes and shoot up through his body. He was almost breathless. Mallory had identified the original quilt. Jessie Frémont had held this quilt. John Frémont had held it. He felt the same thrill he'd felt when he'd seen the Kit Carson letters.

"It's fantastic," Mallory added, "and it ought to be in a museum right now."

"Young lady," Mr. Smith said. "I'm absolutely gobsmacked. This makes me remember that years ago that's what Cornelius said when he first saw the quilt — he swore it had to be the original. But I'd had the story about the fire told to me so many times I just couldn't see straight, I guess.

"I'll call this Phillipa Paxton immediately and invite her to see it; if she thinks you're right, I'll send it off to have it authenticated by experts," he added. "If they agree with you, I'll donate it to a museum immediately. But any notations or signs will have to identify you and Cornelius Patterson for your superior acumen and intuition."

"But how could this happen?" Pete asked. "Why would someone claim this quilt had burned up and then later say it was just a copy of the original?"

"You'd be surprised," Lyle Smith said, "but that sort of thing happens all the time in the underground art market. My guess would be that the fire created such a commotion that someone stole the quilt, which was later presumed to be lost. The thief couldn't sell the original without revealing the theft, so he or she had to settle for claiming it was a replica."

The whole morning had turned out to be even more exciting than Pete had anticipated, and after they had thanked Lyle Smith, given him Phillipa Paxton's phone number, and promised to be in touch, they piled back into the truck, all talking at once. They explained what had happened to Leif, who started driving toward Daniel Hernández's university. Pete could see that Mallory was basking in the afterglow of her discovery.

"Mallory," he said, "if you could see right away that the quilt was original, maybe you'll also be able to see if Hernández's letter is a fake."

"Oh, no," she said. "I couldn't tell anything about a written document. I could feel the quilt and look at the artistry in its design and execution, but there's nothing like that in a piece of paper – especially in a copy of a piece of paper. I think it's interesting that your case has developed into a study of oppositions."

At the word "oppositions," Jupiter sat up straighter. "Could you explain what you mean?" he asked.

"Well," Mallory said, "at the center of your investigations is a quilt supposed to be a copy of the original – or a fake, if you will – and a letter supposed to be real, but actually a fake."

Pete smiled. He thought this was a neat observation, but since Aunt Mathilda had packed a box lunch for the five of them, and

Pete was hungry, at the moment he was more concerned with finding a place to stop and eat. As they passed a small park with picnic tables, he pointed it out, and Leif pulled over.

They ate with little talking, and afterwards Leif drove them to the university. It took a little time to find the building where the History Department was housed, and Pete got anxious that they'd be late, but they finally pulled into a parking spot with fifteen minutes to spare. Pete looked at Jupiter and Bob who both had strange expressions on their faces.

"What's the matter?" he asked. "Didn't lunch agree with you?"

"I'm getting a little worried about sending Mallory on this errand," Jupiter said. "After all, this is a man who we have reason to believe blew up a keg of gunpowder and broke into a college office. Not to mention encouraging a lunatic with a garrote. "

"You don't have to do this if you don't want to," Bob said.

Pete looked at Mallory, who wore an expression of supreme confidence.

"Don't worry about me," she said. "I'm really looking forward to it. I've never met a professional forger. And anyway, if things go wrong, I always carry a dagger in my boot."

Wow! Pete thought. Mallory got out of the truck and started walking away. Pete stared after her, impressed. Then he stared harder. She was wearing sandals.

12

Mallory Aces The Test

As Mallory walked briskly away from the truck, she didn't feel as confident as she'd pretended she felt. Of course, she wasn't worried that Daniel Hernández would actually harm her, but she *was* a little concerned that he would see through her story.

Although she knew she seemed older than she really was, she didn't have much experience in deception, and if she wasn't successful in her attempt to lull Daniel Hernández into letting down his guard, she'd fail in her mission. She was also a little apprehensive that, at the crucial instant, she'd bottle it.

And while technically her mission was simply to extract a copy of a letter that had probably been forged, more importantly, in her mind, it was to impress The Three Investigators – and particularly Jupiter. Convincing his Aunt Mathilda to hire her at the Salvage Yard had been nothing compared with the task of convincing Jupiter she could be trusted with Three Investigators' business.

The door to Daniel Hernández's office

was slightly ajar, but Mallory paused before knocking. According to her watch, she had three minutes until her scheduled appointment. She closed her eyes and focused on what she wanted to achieve – she hoped to walk away with a facsimile of the letter Hernández had supposedly discovered, and she needed to give the impression that she was acting entirely on her own.

When she had called Hernández to set up this appointment, she had told him that while she would soon be a freshman in high school, she was thinking of eventually applying to his university so she could study American history with him. He had asked her if she was from Scotland, and she had said she was. She took a deep breath and knocked.

"Come in," Daniel Hernández said. She pushed the door open and stepped inside.

The office was large, with a window looking out on the quadrangle below. The office walls were crowded with metal bookshelves and posters and photographs – among them a poster for *Bear Valley* and quite a few photos of the man who now rose from his desk chair to meet her.

On the desk, a laptop computer was hooked to a cinema display, but at the moment the screen was black — though it reflected Hernández himself in its glossy, glassy surface. Hernández was wearing a navy sports coat over an open-necked button-down white shirt, a pair of jeans, and loafers. He looked exactly as she had thought he would — the cultivated image of a hip, relaxed young professor.

Mallory stepped forward and held out her hand. "Dr. Hernández," she said. "I'm Mallory MacLeod. It's very nice of you to meet me on such short notice. As I said when we spoke, I'm entering high school in the fall. I've just arrived from Scotland, and I'm already thinking ahead to my college years."

"That's very wise of you," Dr. Hernández said. "Please sit down, Mallory. May I call you Mallory?"

"Sure," Mallory said. She tried to settle back in the chair, to give no hint of the tension she felt. Now that she was in Hernández's office, she was even more worried that she might either lose her nerve or give herself away.

"You said you'd been reading *Manifest Murder*? How did you run across it to begin with?" asked Dr. Hernández.

"My mother has a copy she borrowed from Richard Black. She's working as an assistant costume designer on *Bear Valley*. Her name is Alexandra MacLeod."

"I don't think I've met her," Dr. Hernández said. "But that explains that."

"She's working behind the scenes," Mallory said. "Anyway, I was reading the parts of your book that deal with Kit Carson. I've been fascinated by his story ever since I was a young girl."

Hernández looked surprised.

"I'm amazed you ever even heard of him, growing up in Scotland."

"I was born in California, which is why we moved back here," Mallory said. "And anyway, lots of Brits are obsessed with cowboys and Indians. American westerns have a lot to do with it, of course, but the fascination goes all the way back to the 19th century when men like George Catlin brought over bands of Native Americans and Buffalo Bill Cody brought his traveling Wild West show to England."

"I'm impressed," Dr. Hernández said. "You know a lot more than most freshman in high school in America."

Mallory felt cautiously optimistic. It looked like her Internet cramming the night before might be paying off.

"Lots of the kids I grew up with knew all

about Daniel Boone and Wild Bill Hickok and Billy the Kid and Kit Carson," she said. She was amazed at how easy it was to tell a total lie.

Hernández sat back in his chair. "I was actually doing research on John Frémont," he said, "when I discovered how important Carson had been to his story."

"It just doesn't seem right that he would shoot three unarmed Mexicans in cold blood," Mallory said sadly. At least, she *hoped* it was sadly − and from what Hernández said next, he appeared to have accepted it as just exactly that.

"Well," Hernández said soothingly. "We can't blame Carson too much, after all. He was a military man at the time, and he was just following orders. It's John Frémont we should blame."

"Yes," Mallory said. "John Frémont seems to have deserved to lose the 1856 Presidential election."

"I must say it's bracing to speak to someone so young who has such a firm grasp of history," Hernández said.

"I've always been interested in the past," Mallory said. "It's hard not to be when you grow up in a place where the past is all around

you. I'm fascinated by material culture, and if I
don't study American history in college, I'm
going to study that, instead."

"Oh no!" said Daniel Hernández.
"What can I do to convince you to stick with
your first choice?"

She decided to press her advantage. "I
hadn't really thought about this before," she
said, "but real letters – letters written by hand,
or on a typewriter – are a sort of material culture, aren't they?"

"Yes," Hernández said. "I suppose they
are. And each is one of a kind."

"It would be fascinating to see the letter
you discovered," she added. "Do you have it
here in your office?'

"Alas, no," Hernández said. "It's too
valuable. All I have here is a copy."

"Even that would be great," Mallory
said. "I read the text of the letter in your book,
but as far as I can see, you haven't even posted
a JPG of it on your website."

"You've been to my website?" Hernández asked with pleasure.

"Of course," Mallory said. "That's why
I decided I wanted to study with you!" she
added.

Hernández seemed quite susceptible to

flattery; he smiled broadly and started looking through a stack of papers on his desk.

"I thought I had a copy right here, but I seem to have taken the folder home," he said. "Still, I can print another one. I have a JPG on my computer. Just give me a minute. Oh, wait, perhaps I put that folder in my filing cabinet."

He got up and walked across the room to a cabinet in the corner. As he stood, he jarred his desk, and, at the vibration, the display connected to Hernández's computer popped into bright blue life without Hernández noticing what had happened.

In fact, he was off in the corner with his back to the desk as Mallory began to study the display. She'd been pretty excited at how well she'd been doing with convincing Hernández she was a true admirer, but what happened now was a stroke of fantastic luck. Dr. Hernández had apparently put his computer to sleep – probably when she got there – without closing an open window on his browser. When his computer woke up, the open window was right there – and open to OUTLAW's Facebook page.

Not only that, but as Mallory sat, hardly breathing, studying what she saw, it was clear that Hernández had just finished a post – a post signed not by Daniel Hernández but by someone named Honon Miwok. Although Mallory knew very little about Facebook, she *did* know that when you opened an account on that platform, you were supposed to use your own name, and Hernández was clearly pretending to be someone else.

She scanned the post as quickly as she could and read enough to see that Miwok was thanking his fellow OUTLAWs for raising the bail money for someone who'd been arrested – and that that someone was Dasan Coyote, the guy with the garrote. Mallory had just a minute to reflect that this was important information when, off in the corner, Daniel Hernández found the folder he was looking for and said, with satisfaction, "Here it is!"

Mallory got to her feet and hurried over to stand next to him and peer at it over his arm – knowing that when he turned back to his desk, he'd see that his computer had come to life, but hoping he'd assume it had happened when *she* got up, not when *he* had.

Luckily, that was exactly what he assumed.

"Let's take it back to the desk," he said. He walked across the room in front of her and casually shut the browser window before hand-ing her the document. He smiled broadly.

Mallory took it and studied it. The hand-writing was irregular, but it was the letter Jupiter was looking for. Mallory felt so excited she didn't have to feign it when she said, "Wow. Thanks a lot. This is a real piece of American history."

"Yes, it is," Dr. Hernández said. "It proves a rumor that has hung over John Frémont's reputation for almost a hundred eighty years."

"But I still like Kit Carson," Mallory said.

"And you have every reason to like him," Hernández reassured her. "We all need heroes."

"I agree," Mallory said. "Who are yours?"

"My heroes?" Hernández asked, surprised. "Well – I look up to – "

Mallory glanced at her watch. "Good grief," she said. "I certainly didn't mean to take up this much of your time. I'd better get my skates on." She held up the letter. "May I keep this? At least until I see you again?"

"I – " Hernández began. He smiled. "Why not? I hope it will inspire you to do your own research."

Mallory thrust the letter into her shoulder bag, shook his hand firmly, and looked him straight in the eye. "This is brilliant," she said. "Thank you again. I'll see you in four years, when I graduate from high school."

Unless, of course, you're still in jail, she thought, smiling to herself.

Back in the truck, the boys were waiting eagerly for her.

"How did it go?" Bob asked.

"Fantastically," Mallory said. "Here's the letter."

She handed it to Jupiter who looked at it quickly but thoroughly.

"Great work, Mallory," he said. "I can say without fear of contradiction that, except for the Carson signature, this is written in an entirely different hand than the one in Dr. Paxton's possession."

He handed the paper to Bob who handed it to Pete.

"But that's not even the best thing," Mallory said. "When he was getting up from his desk to pull this out of a filing cabinet, Dr. Hernández bumped his computer display, and when it came on, there was a window open to OUTLAW's Facebook page."

"No way!" Pete said.

"You've got to be kidding!" Bob said.

"Not only that, but he was writing a new post about the garrote guy and signing it as someone named Honon Miwok!" She was happy to find that she remembered this rather unusual name.

"I knew it!" Jupiter said excitedly. Then Mallory and Leif sat watching as Jupiter, Pete, and Bob started leaping around inside the truck, or leaping as much as a truck made possible. They hooted and hollered and finally settled down.

Mallory was thrilled to have been the cause of such jubilation, but she felt she should say, "I didn't think it was *that* exciting."

"Oh, but it is," Jupiter said. "We were right in our suppositions. Dr. Hernández was stuck in a low-paying low-ranking job until he figured out that he needed to publish something dramatic and explosive – and in line with the current historical orthodoxy – if he wanted to get ahead."

"And if we're right," Bob added, "then what he did was go searching for someone in the historical record – someone important enough to matter, and someone about whom people disagreed. Someone who might plausibly fit the role of historical villain."

"Wow," Mallory said. "This is an exciting story. It's like a mystery thriller."

"You can say that again!" Pete said. "This Honon Miwok is a totally fictional character created by Dr. Daniel Hernández!"

Jupiter added, "As far as I can remember, every single post by Honon Miwok made accusations against John Frémont – all of them based on a letter Hernández himself wrote!"

"I don't really think Hernández believes Frémont did anything wrong," Bob agreed. "As far as I can see, Dr. Hernández is just a hypocrite trying to get ahead."

"When I asked him, he also couldn't come up with a single person he actually admired," Mallory said as she stared out the windshield at the cars whizzing by on the freeway.

She didn't think she'd ever get used to the traffic in southern California, and why should she? Although oleanders bloomed on the medium, there were high staggered walls on either side of the highway which had been built to shield the closest houses from the roar of automobiles. It was all too close and frantic, and Mallory found she was looking forward to getting back to Rocky Beach – which suddenly felt a bit like a safe haven.

Leif got off the freeway at the proper exit, and soon they passed the WELCOME TO ROCKY BEACH sign.

"So I think I should drop Mallory off first," Leif said, "before Pete. And then we go back to the Yard, yes?"

But the closer they got to the Wessex House, the more Mallory found herself wishing the day could go on a bit longer. She also kept thinking there was something else she should have told them about her meeting with Daniel Hernández – some point she had meant to share with them but had swept past in the excitement of the moment.

When Leif pulled up next to the boarding house, Pete said, "This is where you live? What a cool old place."

"There aren't many Victorians like this left in Rocky Beach," Jupiter said.

"I bet it was really something before the owner broke it up into apartments," Mallory said. "But it's still pretty great. Of course, we're only living here until our house in Scotland sells. Or until we go back to Scotland."

She paused and then took the plunge. "Would you like to come in for a minute?"

"Absolutely," Bob said.

"I sure would," Pete agreed.

All of them climbed the steps to the porch − even Leif. Mallory led the way down the narrow hall to the apartment and unlocked the door.

Sun streamed in through the sheer curtains over the bay window in the living room, through small leaded stained-glass ornaments hung from the window frames, casting spangling colors everywhere. The air was blessedly cool. Mallory's mother had left a circulating fan on, and as it turned from side to side, streams of air flowed around her.

Mallory was glad her mother had insisted that she take all her things back to her room the night before, so her books and papers and extra clothes had all been tidied away. Now that Mallory was seeing the apartment through the eyes of someone who'd never been there before, it looked − well − quite nice.

The mahogany sheen of the antique dining table caught the light and the plants her mother fussed over − ferns and twining ivy and the banana tree they'd inherited from the previous occupant − looked cheerful and very green.

"Wow!" Pete said. "These are awesome." He was examining some photographs that Mallory and her mother had hung on the walls.

"Those are pictures I took in Scotland," Mallory said. "That's Edinburgh Castle, and that's Ben Nevis, the highest mountain in the British Isles. It's in the Grampians, in what they call the Highlands."

"It's pretty big," Pete said.

"It's only four thousand feet," Mallory said. "But it's big for over there."

Bob and Jupiter were also engrossed. Bob was looking at books in the bookcases, while Jupiter had picked up and was examining an antique dagger sheath made of leather and banded with ornately worked silver. The dagger had been her father's and Mallory had inherited it when he had died, but Jupiter was treating it so respectfully that she didn't object to him noticing it.

Bob turned to Mallory. "It seems like you and your mom have lived here a long time, but it's only been a few months," he said.

Mallory nodded. "It's beginning to feel like home," she said. She hadn't known what it would be like to have Bob and Pete and Jupiter in the apartment, but it felt natural.

"Are any of you guys thirsty?" she asked.

"Yeah," Pete said. "As long as it doesn't have pomegranate in it."

Mallory laughed. "I don't know what's in

the fridge, but help yourselves."

Jupiter stuck to tap water and settled himself in an easy chair; all the others grabbed a soda. The small talk died down, and Mallory could see that Bob and Pete were now waiting for Jupiter to say something – as if he'd given a mysterious signal only they could understand. She noticed he was pinching his bottom lip.

"So, Jupe," asked Bob. "What do you think? Is there any way we can get this guy? Pete's father was right about him all along."

"Yes," Jupiter said. "It's a shame the historical record is so often incomplete or in dispute. That allows people like Daniel Hernández to use it for their own purposes. What really happened when those three Mexicans reached San Rafael? We'll never know. But ten years later, when John Frémont was running for President, his enemies didn't let that stop them. Two articles were published in a Los Angeles newspaper claiming that the Mexicans were killed under Frémont's explicit orders."

"That was pretty explosive stuff," Mallory said. "Imagine someone running for President today who was accused of murder."

"Today, with the Internet mobs," Bob said, "it wouldn't have to be murder. Some stupid thing he did in high school could ruin his whole life. Even if he didn't actually do it."

"Still," Jupiter went on, "with Frémont there was no – as they say – smoking gun. So Hernández saw his chance to manufacture one. He'd forge a letter from Kit Carson that indirectly charged Frémont with the murders. Brilliant. And he could do that without involving anyone else because of his background in calligraphy. He could use a nibbed pen really well, and the only thing he'd really have to get perfect was seven small letters – C Carson. The signature was good enough to fool a handwriting expert, and Hernández went on to publish his blockbuster article."

"That sure took a lot of nerve," Pete said.

"He's one cool customer," Mallory said. "He may even have started to believe he could never be caught."

"I don't think he's gotten quite that far," Bob said. "Or he wouldn't be trying to get his hands on Phillipa Paxton's Carson letter."

"That's right," Jupiter said. "When he came up with his plan, he had no way of knowing that another historian owned a real Carson letter dated the same day as his fake one. So when he read about the movie, and then read Dr. Paxton's book, he realized he had a problem. If enough people paid attention to the movie and to Dr. Paxton's book, they'd stumble on the contradiction, just the way we have."

"You almost have to feel sorry for him," Pete said.

"Almost," Bob said. "But not quite."

"Let me see if I've got this all straight," Mallory said. "He approached Dr. Paxton, all buddy-buddy, trying to buy her Carson letters. When that didn't work, and he found out she was looking for the flag quilt, he tracked down Lyle Smith."

"Right," Pete said. "He thought that if he could get the quilt, he might barter it for the letters."

"Meanwhile," Jupiter said, "this OUTLAW group had been forming, and one of his own students was a member. A guy he must have known, from teaching him, was really crazy. So he made up this Miwok Indian named Honon Miwok and wrote posts on their page, getting them all riled up about John Frémont. All in order to have them threaten and frighten Dr. Paxton and provide a smoke screen for him breaking into her office and stealing her letter. He knew that both she and the police would blame the office break-in on OUTLAW."

"Yes," Bob said. "A classic example of misdirection."

Mallory understood in a way she hadn't before how The Three Investigators worked. It was great to see. In particular, she was impressed with Jupiter's deductions. Although she'd been eager to impress him before she ever even met him, for the first time she saw the depth of his intelligence and insight and why Pete and Bob respected him so much. She didn't know how to say that, though – or even if she wanted to.

"So," she finally said. "It sounds like you've pretty much wrapped this up."

"Yes and no," Jupiter said. "We understand what happened and we understand why it happened. But as far as I can see, we can't prove any of it. I'm really glad you managed to get a copy of the letter, but knowing it's a forgery and proving it are two different things. Even the two different hands and the two different locations on the same day aren't proof.

"Clearly, the letters can't *both* be real, but since Dr. Paxton has never had hers authenticated, and Dr. Hernández has, why shouldn't *hers* be the forgery? Also, even if we *could* prove his was forged, that still doesn't prove that Hernández forged it," Jupiter said.

"Couldn't experts date the paper or the ink?" Bob asked. "The way they're going to date the flag quilt? That would show he used contemporary materials to fake a 19th-century document."

"Maybe," Jupiter said, "but I wouldn't count on it. He's too clever; I'm sure he would have thought of that. And besides, there's no way he'd give it to those experts with nothing to force him but our word. Still, we've got to find a way to expose Hernández – to keep him from messing with the truth, falsifying history, and lying to students."

Finally Mallory figured out what to say. "I see why you're the First Investigator," she told Jupiter.

"Thank you," Jupiter said, smiling. "And let me return the compliment, if I may. What you did up in Auburn, with your memory – well, that was based on an innate ability you have that others don't. But what you did with Daniel Hernández – that took real courage and real talent. You managed to fool a very clever man, and to get from him something he's kept closely guarded. You also took advantage of a sudden opportunity to see what he's been up to on OUTLAW's Facebook page. Congratulations."

Next to him, Bob grinned broadly.

"Jupiter," Leif said from where he was sitting on the couch. "I do not think I should be gone from work any longer. I need to take the truck back."

Pete leapt to his feet and he, Bob, and Jupiter told Mallory how much fun they'd had with her at Lyle Smith's and what a great job she'd done with Hernández. And then they were gone.

Mallory stood on the porch, watching them drive away, sorry to see them go but filled with a feeling of genuine contentment. She really liked them, all of them, but it was more than that — she liked using her intelligence in the service of something honest and good. Although she hadn't yet had to use her own deductive reasoning in the course of solving a real life mystery, she'd helped The Three Investigators in other ways twice now, and if she kept being able to help them, maybe, at some time in the future, she'd become — oh, she didn't know quite what.

Looked at realistically, she'd never want to be an actual "investigator." For one thing, it was an illogical concept. After all, if *anyone* joined The Three Investigators, there'd be four investigators, not three. Even more important was the fact that Pete, Bob, and Jupiter had known each other since kindergarten, and you could never hope to become the same kind of friend with someone you met when you were entering high school as you could with someone you'd known since you were five.

That was why she'd kicked and screamed as hard as she had when her mother had told her they were moving to Rocky Beach. Back home in Scotland, she'd had a couple of long-term friends of her own, and making new friends at her age – she was almost fourteen – had seemed a difficult prospect. Now, it didn't seem quite as hard, and Mallory thought that having Pete and Bob and Jupiter as friends might be something she could accomplish.

Mallory turned and went back into her apartment, and then into her bedroom where she took off her shoes and lay down on her bed, propping her head on several pillows. When she and her mother had been at the Scottish music camp outside of Grass Valley, she'd taken part in a game called Icons of Scotland. Since it had involved nothing more than remembering the order of a series of flashed images of things like Balmoral Castle or Sean Connery, she'd found it easy, and her skill had caused her team to win.

The prize had been a rubber model of the Loch Ness monster, and Mallory now kept Nessie on her bedside table. The monster had a long green neck and a small green head with reddish eyes and looked a lot like a brontosaurus.

Ever since the evening she'd won it, Mallory had been strangely fond of it. She'd never thought of herself as someone who needed a lot of approval from other people, but when everyone had applauded at the end of the Icons of Scotland game, she'd liked it a lot.

Mallory lifted Nessie down and stared into her eyes, thinking again about the day. Though, in a way, Jupiter had been onto something when he'd said that her visual memory was an innate ability, she actually spent a good deal of time purposely remembering things.

For that reason, as she lay holding Nessie, she thought back on everything that had just happened, and when she got to the scene in Daniel Hernández's office, she suddenly remembered that although she'd told the boys that Dr. Hernández was pretending to be Ho-non Miwok, she *hadn't* told them that the post Hernández was writing had thanked his fellow OUTLAWs for raising the bail money for the guy calling himself Dasan Coyote.

Oh, well, it probably wasn't all that important, she thought. So this Dasan Coyote would be out of jail soon. So what?

13

Hitting Pay Dirt

Almost as soon as the three boys jumped into the truck with Leif, Jupiter starting thinking hard. He was pleased − and relieved − at how well things had gone with Mallory and Daniel Hernández, and it was crucial that they now knew what Hernández's Kit Carson letter actually looked like. Still, Jupiter had been telling the truth when he'd said that knowing something was a forgery and proving it beyond a reasonable doubt were two different things.

"When we get back to Headquarters," Bob said, "let's call Dr. Paxton. She'll be stunned when we tell her about the quilt and the letter."

Jupiter agreed. If Dr. Paxton had been excited by the idea of a copy of the commemorative flag quilt, she would be beside herself when they told her they'd uncovered the original − even if it wasn't for sale.

As for Daniel Hernández, Dr. Paxton would surely be very relieved when she learned that everything that had been happening to her had a logical explanation. Nevertheless, until

Jupiter could figure out how to prove what he had to prove, he didn't want to get in touch with Dr. Paxton again.

"I think we should put that off," he said. "In fact, you guys should go home and have some dinner, and then come over later. I've got some thinking to do, and it would probably be better if I did it by myself."

Leif dropped Pete at his house, then drove to the Salvage Yard where Bob had left his bicycle.

"You sure I can't help?" Bob asked Jupiter.

"I'm sure, Records," Jupiter said. "I need to think about how we can prove this letter that Hernández supposedly 'discovered' is a forgery. You think about it, too. We'll put our heads together later."

"O.K.," Bob said, and he took off for home. Jupiter watched him ride away, then went to his house where he found that his Aunt Mathilda had dinner waiting.

He ate quickly, thanked her, then made his way to Headquarters. He booted up the firm's computer and started by doing searches for famous forgeries − trying to find out if they were connected by a common thread. Maybe he'd start a new Facebook group: Outing Forgers From Past and Present Centuries. OUTFORGE. He liked it.

As he researched, Jupiter was astounded by how many famous forgeries there were and how long it had taken for some of them to be found out. Indeed, it almost looked as though there were two realities – one filled with objects and a parallel one filled with forgeries of those objects. And really, Daniel Hernández's forgery was, in the historical record, pretty small potatoes.

For example, the Roman Emperor Constantine, who ruled in the early years of the fourth century, supposedly wrote a document giving the city of Rome and most of western Europe to the head of the Catholic church. Now that, Jupiter thought, was audacious. The document wasn't proven to be a forgery for almost eleven hundred years.

The eighteenth century was a banner year for forgeries, Jupiter discovered. A poet by the name of James McPherson found in the Highlands of Scotland an entire cycle of epic poems, written in the third century by a blind bard named Ossian. McPherson had "translated" the poems from Gaelic and published them to much acclaim – fooling many famous poets of the day. But, of course, as it turned out, he'd written them himself.

Jupiter found himself thinking that he'd have to tell Mallory about Ossian McPherson, and then he shook his head a little grimly. If he was thinking of sharing something like this with her, clearly his feelings about Mallory were changing – and that was something he had no time for, at the moment.

Going back to his work, Jupiter also discovered that in London in 1790, a man named William Henry Ireland claimed to have "discovered" – just like Hernández – two lost plays by Shakespeare. It seemed that forgers, in general, were motivated by greed and power, so Daniel Hernández was in good company – though document forgers were generally tripped up because they had made a mistake of some kind.

So what mistake had Hernández made? He might be very clever, but he was not infallible, Jupiter thought.

The copy of the Carson letter that Mallory had gotten from Hernández lay on the desk, and Jupiter found himself staring first at it and then at his research. Some forgeries were easy to spot because they were crudely done, but the best ones were uncovered because they had gotten a historical fact wrong or because they had —

Jupiter stared at the letter in front of him. Obviously, the language Kit Carson had used in the letters he had dictated in the 1800s was different from the language he would have used if he were writing letters today, Jupiter thought. If Daniel Hernández had made an obvious blunder in the letter he had faked, — if, for example, he had had Carson stop at a corner store for a soda — no one would have been fooled for a second. The references to a corner store and a soda would have been blatant anachronisms.

But what if Hernández had made a blunder that wasn't so obvious? What if he had used a word or a term that had sounded right to him when he wrote it, but that people hadn't actually been using in 1846, when the letter was supposedly written? If he'd used a word or a term that no one then had ever heard, then Jupiter didn't need microscopes and chemicals; all he needed was a dictionary.

After all, dictionaries were chock full of information — not just about what a word meant, or how it was used in a sentence, but about how it had come into being, moving from one language — like Greek or Latin or Middle English — to another. Also, most dictionaries gave an indication of the first time a word or words had been used. Jupiter studied the supposed Carson letter carefully. Was there anything that seemed wrong?

To the attention of John Charles Frémont:

You have asked for a report and here it is. Although I had some questions about the propriety of leaving the two surviving female settlers in a settlement so dominated by men, I accepted your suggestion that to bring them with us would involve arduous toil.

After seeing them securely quartered, I engaged in some mercantile pursuits and provided myself with a suitable horse. In truth, I hit pay dirt by obtaining a magnificent chestnut mare.

We were all well armed and mounted and set out with the first light of morning. With pleasant weather and no enemy to fear, we should have reached our destination in a long day's ride.

Instead, we encountered hostile Indians, and after killing three of them, drove the others off. Some Mexicans we met were also killed. I assumed you would not object, since when we encountered Don José Berreyesa and the sons of Don Francisco de Haro near the shores of San Rafael, you told me we had no room for prisoners.

The one day stretched to two as a result of our encounters, but we are now safely in the Fort.
C Carson.

On a pad of paper, Jupiter wrote down any word or phrase he wondered about, then began looking them up, one after another.

"Arduous" meant difficult, or requiring a lot of effort; it dated from the 16th century and came from a Latin word meaning "steep or difficult." "Toil," of course, meant especially hard work and also came from the Latin. So nothing there – though Jupiter noted that Hernández was a bit redundant, since "toil" all by itself meant difficult work and probably didn't need "arduous" at all.

"Mercantile" meant related to trade or commerce and dated from the mid-17th century. It came from the Italian word for "merchant." Jupiter didn't even bother to look up "pursuits." That seemed as though it had been around forever.

So far, so bad.

He went back to the letter. What about sentence structure? In his other letters, had Carson dictated sentences as long and complicated as some in this one? He had to assume that Hernández would be at least that clever. And he spent a moment admiring the word choice. "With pleasant weather and no enemy to fear" certainly gave the sense of having been written in 1846.

Jupiter was stumped. Was this one of those very few forgeries with no mistakes? Was Hernández going to get away with it? He pinched his bottom lip hard and went back to reading. Carson had had doubts about leaving the two unaccompanied women, who were under his protection, among so many men, but he'd come to see that Frémont was right in saying that it would be too difficult to bring them along. After he thought they were safe, he'd bought some stuff, and one of the things he'd bought was a chestnut mare − a horse he seemed really happy with. In fact, he said he'd "hit pay dirt" − which meant that he'd found something really valuable.

From their previous case, in the Gold Country, Jupiter knew the phrase referred to miners having arrived at a level where there was enough ore in the soil to make mining profitable. In other words, it was dirt that paid. Then he stopped and his heart began to pound. Hard. Gold had been discovered in California in 1848 And the fake Kit Carson letter had supposedly been written in 1846.

With a mounting sense of excitement, Jupiter checked various online dictionaries to make certain. Sure enough, the phrase "hit pay dirt" had only come into common use several years *after* the physical activity it described. This seemed to prove that Jupiter himself had hit pay dirt. Carson *couldn't* have used the phrase "hit pay dirt" in 1846, because it hadn't yet entered the English language in the United States!

And then, just as Jupiter was experiencing a sense of exhilaration, he remembered that simply because the letter had been forged did not mean that Daniel Hernández himself had forged it. Jupiter knew he had, but he still had to prove it.

He heard a rattle outside, and then footsteps, and then some banging, and then Pete and Bob spilled into Headquarters. Before they had even had a chance to sit down, Jupiter said, "I found it. Hernández used a phrase in the letter which hadn't entered the language in 1846." He explained what the phrase was.

There was general jubilation inside Headquarters. Fist-bumps flew everywhere. Then Jupiter settled his two friends down and told them they still had to figure out a way to pin this on Daniel Hernández.

"He'll deny it, of course," Jupiter said. "He'll say that if the letter is really a forgery he didn't know it; he'll say that he went to the trouble of getting the signature authenticated. His only crime was finding the letter in an obscure book in an obscure bookstore.”

“But we can’t let him get away with it!” Pete said. “People got hurt! Dr. Paxton’s office door was trashed and her tires were slashed and she had to get stitches.”

“Not to mention her anxiety attacks and sleepless nights,” Bob said.

“And he betrayed his students,” Jupiter said. “He lied to them and used them. He besmirched a long-dead man’s reputation. Worst of all, he falsified the historical record. Human progress is based on the belief that in every generation people add to the truth, not cover it over with lies.”

“Maybe we can lay a trap for him!” Pete said excitedly.

“What kind of a trap?” Jupiter asked.

“Well, we know he’s still got Dr. Paxton’s letter on the brain,” Pete said, “or he wouldn’t have been sneaking around her garage door leaving footprints. If he was desperate enough to break into her office, he might be desperate enough to break into her house. And we could catch him.”

“That’s an excellent idea, Second,” Jupiter said. “But we can’t sit around and wait for him to try it. We'd have to force the issue."

"Maybe we could send him an e-mail saying we know his letter is fake," Pete suggested. "Not from us, of course. It would have to be anonymous. That might push him. We wouldn't say why we know the letter's a fake, so he'd still think that if he got his hands on Dr. Paxton's letter, and destroyed it, he'd be safe."

"But don't you think we ought to ask Dr. Paxton?" Bob said. "After all, it's her house he'd be breaking into."

"Let's call her," Pete said.

Bob got out Dr. Paxton's cellphone number, after which Jupiter dialed it, then hit SPEAKER.

When Phillipa Paxton picked up, Jupiter said, "Jupiter Jones here, Dr. Paxton. Together with Pete and Bob. We have news for you."

"Jupiter!" Dr. Paxton said. "How wonderful to hear from you."

"Have you heard from a Mr. Lyle Smith?" Jupiter asked.

"No," she said. "Why?"

"He's the man who lived in Sonoma in 1998, in that house you gave us the picture of. The three of us visited him yesterday in Sherman Oaks, with our friend Mallory MacLeod."

"So you found the replica flag quilt?" she asked.

"Better than that, actually," Jupiter said. "Mallory, who tends to know about these things, thinks that the quilt Mr. Smith owns was made in 1860 and not in 1912. In other words – "

"It's the original quilt!" Dr. Paxton exclaimed. "But how can that be?"

"Lyle Smith suggested that it might have been stolen during the San Francisco fire, and that whoever stole it could only sell it as a reproduction, or they would have had to admit the theft."

"Jupiter," Dr. Paxton said, barely able to keep her voice under control. "I can't tell you how exciting this is. This is a find of great significance."

"And wait until you see it!" Pete said. "It's amazing."

"And there's more good news," Jupiter went on. "We've found incriminating evidence against Daniel Hernández. This whole thing has been about a letter supposedly written by Kit Carson that Hernández pretended he had found but that he had really forged. Unfortunately for him, he chose badly when he dated the letter – it's dated the same day as one of your original Carson letters. Hernández has been trying to get his hands on your letter to destroy it — so that no one will question the authenticity of his forgery."

"Oh my goodness," Dr. Paxton said. "Let me sit down."

Jupiter explained to her how they wanted to catch Hernández in the act of trying to steal her Carson letter — how they'd alarm him and get him to act. Dr. Paxton immediately agreed to the plan.

"If we can catch him in my house, that will be the end of him," she said triumphantly.

"But he'll have to believe you aren't there," Jupiter said, "or else he'll think it's too risky. I can't believe he would actually try to steal the letter with you in the house."

"Then I won't be here," Dr. Paxton said, "as far as he's concerned. Let me think." She paused a moment. "Why don't I call Richard Black and tell him there's a family emergency that will take me out of town, and I wanted to let him know so that he could be sure to tell Hernández. I'll say that that way we can be certain that there's at least one historian on the set. I'll tell him I'm leaving the day after tomorrow."

"That's good," Jupiter said. "That will give us plenty of time to get all the details of our trap in order."

"If we're going to confront him in the house," Dr. Paxton said, "I'd feel better if Pete's father was with us. I've come to like him a lot, and I totally trust him."

Pete beamed.

"That's right, Dr. Paxton," he said. "You can count on him completely."

"If it's all right with you," Jupiter added, "I'll come the day after tomorrow to look at the house again. The night we expect him to break in, you could leave your front light on so it would force him around the back. He won't try the garage door, I don't think; it's too visible and would make too much noise."

"This all sounds terrific, Jupiter," Dr. Paxton said. "Just give me a call before you come."

Jupiter hung up with a feeling of satisfaction. "Pete," he asked. "Do you think your father will be available and willing?"

"I sure do," Pete said. "If it means catching Hernández, my father will be all over it."

"Maybe we should ask Mallory, too," Bob said. "After all, she sure put herself out to help us yesterday."

"Yes, she did," Jupiter said. "And I feel badly about that now. We put her at some risk when there was no real reason to. If I'd thought it all through carefully enough, I'd have looked for an anachronism in the letter before I did anything else."

Seeing the expression on Pete's face, he added, "An anachronism is just somebody putting a custom or an object or a phrase into a historical period it doesn't belong in."

"That won't matter to Mallory," Bob said. "She loves a good adventure. And besides, part of what she found out − about Hernández being Honon Miwok − couldn't have been found out anywhere but in his office."

"That's true," Jupiter said. "Of course we should invite her. Though it's possible her mother won't let her come. Mrs. MacLeod might not see any reason for her to be present at what might be considered a slightly dangerous occasion."

"I'll send her an e-mail," Bob said. "And speaking of e-mails, we still have to write one to Hernández."

"Yes," said Jupiter, "and I've been thinking. If it's just an anonymous letter saying

273

the author knows Hernández is a forger, it might just alarm him. I think we should write the letter from someone who isn't threatening or accusing but just puzzled by this strange coincidence of two letters with the same date being written from different places. The letter could express concern that perhaps Hernández has been fooled – rather than accusing him of trying to do the fooling."

"That's very smart," Bob said. "Let's do it." He sat in the desk chair, and after a little research about names that meant "secretive," opened a Gmail account using the name Dr. Bian Menteuse.

"*Bian* is a Vietnamese name meaning secretive, and *menteuse* is the French word for liar," Bob explained.

"That's good," Jupiter said. "Very funny."

"Don't you think he'll be suspicious of that name?" Pete asked.

"Not at all," Jupiter said.

"You know," Bob said. "I just realized that we don't think it's O.K. for Dr. Hernández to pretend to be Honon Miwok, but it's O.K. for me to pretend to be Dr. Bian Menteuse."

"Yeah," Pete said. "And it's O.K. for

Dr. Paxton to lie to the director about being out of town, but not O.K. for Dr. Hernández to lie about John Frémont."

Jupiter smiled. His friends were right, of course. "I have to admit that the contradictions you bring up are real," he said. "But I still believe that catching and revealing Hernández is for the greater good. I guess it all comes down to motive."

"You mean that our motives are good and his are bad?" Pete said.

"Well, yes," said Jupiter. "We're running a sting, essentially. And we're doing it for what we think are good reasons. Hernández, on the other hand, is doing what he's doing purely for his own sake, and in the process harming others. What we're trying to do is keep him from doing any more harm. We're sifting the truth, as it were."

"Looking for pay dirt!" Pete said, smiling.

"Exactly," Jupiter said. "For pay dirt. And for a dirty scoundrel."

14

The Trap Is Sprung

Two days later, Bob was in Phillipa Paxton's white SUV on the way to the Salvage Yard. The early evening sun was a warm gold, spilling over the mesquite and eucalyptus trees and the houses where families were gathering for dinner. Bob and his parents had already eaten by the time Dr. Paxton came to pick him up. His mother and father had come out to meet her; though she and Bob's mother had both taught at Reedmore College for years, they'd never run into one another before. He was glad that they'd seemed to like one another. Maybe they'd become friends.

Dr. Paxton drove with both hands on the wheel, eyes straight forward. She looked calm and composed, but the skin over her cheekbones seemed drawn, and one of her eyes twitched. When Bob tried to talk to her, she smiled quickly and said she was "concentrating on her driving," but Bob knew she was thinking ahead to that evening.

The last two days had been a frantic rush to get everything in place for tonight. Bob

276

had written an e-mail to Hernández in his role as the helpful but puzzled historian Dr. Bian Menteuse and had gotten a curt reply – with just a hint of alarm – in which Hernández had thanked his unknown correspondent and said he'd certainly look into this apparent contradiction.

At the same time, Dr. Paxton had told Richard Black she'd be away for a few days, starting this morning, and to please let Dr. Hernández know. Pete had had no trouble convincing his father to join them; he said his father was really looking forward to it. Bob could feel the circle tightening.

The one piece of disappointing news was that Mallory couldn't come. Bob had e-mailed her, inviting her, and she'd written back to say that her mother had said no – just as Jupiter had predicted. But Bob was looking forward to being able to tell her all about it afterwards.

Dr. Paxton suddenly broke her silence. "Jupiter came over to my house this afternoon," she said. "He seems so much older than thirteen – or even almost fourteen. He was very thorough. Very methodical."

"He has a logical mind," Bob said.

"He wanted to go over all the ways Hernández might break in," Dr. Paxton said.

"He walked me through each one. He was extremely reassuring."

Bob looked at her, her shoulders tense, her knuckles white. "But you weren't reassured," he said.

"Yes, I was," she said. "But at the end of each of Jupiter's scenarios, there was Daniel Hernández, in my house."

"But you won't be alone," Bob said. "We'll all be with you."

Dr. Paxton looked at him, and at last she smiled. "Yes," she said. "I know you will."

She pulled into the Salvage Yard lot and parked. Since Daniel Hernández knew both Dr. Paxton's car and Mr. Crenshaw's truck, Jupe had decided they couldn't risk having either vehicle parked near Dr. Paxton's house. So they'd planned to rendezvous here and all drive over to Dr. Paxton's in one of the Salvage Yard's trucks. Pete and his father had arrived some time earlier, and everyone was waiting by the Salvage Yard's office.

Jupiter was in top form, electric with energy; Bob could practically hear his brain humming. He seemed exhilarated but calm, all his senses on high alert. "Everything's in place," he said. "Uncle Titus has given us his blessing, so Mr. Crenshaw will drive us all over in a Salvage Yard truck. We'll park several blocks away and walk over. We should all plan to be in our positions well ahead of time, even though Dr. Hernández won't try anything until it's dark. Hernández thinks Dr. Paxton's away. So he'll take his time and mostly worry about being seen."

"That sounds right," Mr. Crenshaw said. "Because there's a door from the garage into the house, I wondered if Hernández might try to get in that way," Jupiter said. "But there's a streetlight right in front of Dr. Paxton's house, so the garage door will be brightly lit. Hernández won't risk that. He'll go around to the back where it's totally dark."

This made sense to everyone; there were no disagreements.

"Finally," Jupiter said. "It won't be enough just to catch him outside. He'd say he was taking a walk, or was just going to drop by and say hello. He'd come up with a lie very quickly; he's good at that. So we have to catch him actually breaking into the house. Dr. Paxton's back door has a glass panel on the top, and two locks – a deadbolt controlled by a lever on the inside of the door, and a second, keyed lock in the doorknob.

"If Dr. Paxton leaves the keyed lock unlocked and just locks the deadbolt, the odds are good that Daniel Hernández will break the glass, then just stick his hand through and turn the deadbolt."

"Why don't we make it even easier?" Mr. Crenshaw said. "Maybe we should leave the back door completely unlocked." He looked at Dr. Paxton. "As if Phillipa had just forgotten it in her rush to get out of there. That way there won't be anything at all holding Hernández back. What do you think?"

Jupiter looked at Mr. Crenshaw and nodded. "That should work as well," he said.

Bob smiled. He was proud of Jupiter for being flexible and able to compromise.

"Good," Mr. Crenshaw said, clapping his hands together. "So we'll be waiting for him inside. He'll need enough time to reveal his motives – we want him in Phillipa's study, hopefully with the letter in his hands. Maybe she could leave a copy of it somewhere he'd find it easily – after we make sure the original letters are safe."

"Dr. Paxton has already copied the letters and hidden the originals, at my request," Jupiter said. "You and Pete and I can hide in the study, behind Dr. Paxton's desk, and Bob and Dr. Paxton can hide in the living room."

"One last thing," Mr. Crenshaw said. "I don't think this guy's violent, but you never know how someone will react when he's cornered. So I want to make one thing clear right now. The three of you and Dr. Paxton stay well away from Hernández. If anyone needs to tackle him, it'll be me. I don't want any help from any of you. Do you understand?"

Bob had gotten to know Pete's father a good deal better over the last week – particularly during their trip to Sonoma. He was friendly, warm, and easy-going. So the sudden change in his tone was a surprise – he sounded commanding and stern, and Bob understood that Mr. Crenshaw thought there was the possibility of real danger.

"Yes," Bob said. "I think we all understand," and Pete and Jupiter quickly agreed. "Let's go!"

They all piled into the Ram 2500, with Mr. Crenshaw driving. It didn't take long before they reached Dr. Paxton's neighborhood. They walked the last five blocks quickly, without talking. Dr. Paxton's house looked peaceful – hardly the destination of a burglar. The adobe walls with their arched wood-trimmed windows glowed in the fading light and the simple porch with its wood posts holding a clay-tiled roof was already lit by the light Dr. Paxton had left on.

Jupiter raised the garage door and closed and locked it behind them, then led the way to the door into the hall. By then the streetlights had come on. Bob found that everyone was moving quickly and speaking in low tones – almost whispering, as if Daniel Hernández could somehow overhear them. Once they were inside, Jupiter double-locked the door between the garage and the hall and made sure the back door into the kitchen was unlocked. Already the backyard was gathering its pools of inky darkness.

At Jupiter's urging, Dr. Paxton put the copies she had made of the relevant letters in a manila folder on which she'd written CARSON LETTERS with a Sharpie, and Jupiter and Mr. Crenshaw positioned it on her desk, trying as hard as they could to make the placement look casual, even haphazard.

"O.K.," Jupiter said. "Does everyone have a flashlight?"

Everyone nodded. "Get set," Jupiter said. "Go!"

The five of them dispersed to their places, Jupe, Pete, and Mr. Crenshaw to the study, Bob and Dr. Paxton to the living room where they sat behind a sofa. Bob quickly became aware that everything electric or electronic in the house had its own tiny glowing eye, yellow or red or white – the TV's ON button, the control for the air conditioner, even some of the electrical sockets which had little specks of green. They'd left the curtains across the front windows open, and light from the streetlights filtered in. The living room, as it turned out, was far from dark.

"Are you O.K.?" Bob whispered to Dr. Paxton. She smiled at him and nodded. Bob glanced at his watch. Nine o'clock. The sun had set an hour before, and it would soon be as dark outside as it was going to get.

The minutes dragged by and Bob's legs were beginning to cramp when he noticed movement outside. A man was coming down the sidewalk, dressed entirely in black. He was contained and nonchalant, comfortable and coordinated, a natural athlete. He looked to both sides of the street and kept walking, casually, out for an evening stroll. Bob craned his neck but the man was now out of sight. But he would be back. Daniel Hernández was casing the place.

"He's here," he whispered to Dr. Paxton. Though he'd been expecting this – though everything they'd done for the last two days

had been aimed at luring Hernández here –
Bob still could hardly believe it. Everything was
working out just as Jupiter had said it would. It
was amazing how, once you understood who a
person really was, you could predict how he
would act.

Jupiter had been right. Hernández's
book about John Frémont, his outrage at
Frémont's supposed actions, even his sugges-
tions about the script for *Bear Valley* – all of it
was a sham, a pose, nothing other than a calculated bid for recognition and advancement.
He didn't care about the native Americans of
California; he didn't care about anyone but
himself. He had infiltrated OUTLAW and used
its members to cover his own tracks.

And then Bob saw him coming back.
This time he was walking a bit more slowly,
more furtively, and after a quick look around to
make sure no one was watching, he darted to
the side of Phillipa Paxton's house and around
the back. Bob looked at Dr. Paxton whose eyes
were wide open in anticipation and fear.

Bob could feel his heart pick up. He
heard noises in the kitchen, the swish of the
doorstop on the tile floor, the scrape of a chair
as Hernández bumped against it, footsteps.
Hernández had a small flashlight, much like

the ones the boys had, and its bright circle darted here and there.

From his vantage spot behind the sofa, Bob saw the dark figure enter the living room and pause. Bob could see that he was wearing black gloves. He swept the room with the flashlight until he found the door to Dr. Paxton's study and entered it. From a distance, Bob could see the flashlight beam illuminate the surface of Dr. Paxton's desk. There it was, as Bob imagined, right in front of him. A folder marked CARSON LETTERS. He picked it up.

"I *knew* you were a villain," Martín Crenshaw said, rising from behind the desk.

He flicked on a light and lunged for Hernández. Bob saw the astonishment on Hernández's face as he lithely pivoted and headed for the living room. But by then, Bob and Dr. Paxton were on their feet, blocking his exit. When he saw them, he stopped short.

"I don't remember inviting you to my house, Daniel," Dr. Paxton said.

Daniel Hernández was no longer the cool, collected, manipulative man he'd managed to be for so long; his face was white and he looked panicked. Pete, Jupiter, and Mr. Crenshaw were right behind him, and when Hernández turned toward them, Dr. Paxton picked up a heavy book from the coffee table and whacked him on the shoulder with it. He lurched to the left, staggered, and was just in time to meet Martín Crenshaw's fist, which caught him with a clean upper cut. He crumpled to the floor.

In no time, two lamps in the room had been turned on and although the room was still fairly dimly lit, it seemed bright to Bob after the darkness. The five of them stared down at Hernández – who rolled onto his back, fingering his jaw where Mr. Crenshaw had punched him. Blood from his split lip trickled down his chin as he clambered to his feet. Of all of them, Bob saw, Dr. Paxton was the one who was most angry. Once she got started, there was no stopping her.

"You've terrorized me and broken into my house, Daniel, but what's far worse is that you've broken your trust with our discipline and with your students. You've falsified the historical record; and you've not only lied to your students – you've used them. I'm going right to the head of your department, and I'm going to do everything I can to make certain that you never teach again. It won't be hard to prove that you forged the Carson letter you made your name with, and it also won't be hard to

prove that you encouraged this group OUT-
LAW to engage in violence against me. You're
a disgrace, and I'll be proud to do everything I
can to ruin you."

Although blood was still trickling down
Dr. Hernández's chin, there was a thin smile
on his face.

"Do you want me to call Chief Reynolds, Dad?" Pete asked his father. Bob could
see that Pete could hardly wait to turn this guy
over to the man who had given The Three Investigators the status of Rocky Beach junior
deputies.

"Yes," Mr. Crenshaw said. "Let's get
the Chief here, pronto."

Hernández smiled more broadly. "I'd
think again, Martín, before you do that. You
and Phillipa here are the only ones who've
committed a crime, and I'm more than ready
to press charges."

"What are you talking about?" Dr. Paxton said.

"All I did," Hernández said, "is enter a
colleague's unlocked door. There's no sign of a
break-in. And nothing has been taken. On the
other hand, the two of you assaulted me, and
even if I can't prove much with Phillipa, I have
this to show the police from you," he said to

Mr. Crenshaw, pointing to his jaw.

Bob saw that the book Dr. Paxton held – the one she had hit Hernández with – was a big coffee table book titled *The Native American Tribes of California*.

Bob looked at Jupiter whose face was a mask of chagrin.

"He's right," Jupiter said. "To accuse someone of breaking and entering, there has to be breaking, not simply entering. It isn't against the law to enter an unlocked door. And Dr. Hernández hadn't actually left the house with anything that didn't belong to him at the time Mr. Crenshaw hit him."

Now it was Mr. Crenshaw's turn to be upset. He slapped himself across the forehead with his palm. "My fault," he said. "My mistake."

"No," Jupiter said. "Your suggestion made sense, and for all we know, it was the lack of a lock that got this miscreant here in the first place. If the door had been locked, he might *not* have broken in. We have no way to know now. "

"As far as I'm concerned," Dr. Paxton said, "it's just as well the Rocky Beach police not get involved – though maybe we could ask the ones up in Sonoma to look a little further into who set off that keg of gunpowder on the set. On this end, I think we have everything we need in order to see that justice is done – by which I mean that the fake Carson letter is discredited, and Dr. Hernández here loses his job. It's more important that he stop teaching and writing nonsense than that he be prosecuted for forgery or burglary."

"That may be so," Bob said. "But that won't stop him from doing again what he did with OUTLAW."

"What do you mean?" Pete asked.

"The explosion he triggered when he lit the fuse on that keg of gunpowder was contained," Bob said. "But he lit another fuse with OUTLAW, and that one keeps exploding and exploding. What's really scary is how easy it was for him to set off the passions of the mob."

"A very astute observation, Second," Jupiter said.

"Get out of my house before I change my mind about calling the authorities," Dr. Paxton added. "Though before you do, I'd like a picture. Just to record the moment – and to be able to prove to Richard Black and the head of your department that you were in my house tonight."

Martín Crenshaw stood right behind Daniel Hernández, ready to restrain him if he moved. Pete stood next to him, and Jupiter and Bob stood on the other side. Dr. Paxton took the picture with her phone – which had a date stamp. Only later, when he saw the photo, did Bob see that Hernández was smoldering with rage and indignation. It was hardly a picture of a bunch of friends. The man in the middle looked like what he was – a criminal apprehended in the middle of a crime.

The boys stepped back and Martín Crenshaw shoved Hernández toward the back door. "Go," he said. "Get out of here."

Hernández strolled away, but he paused in the door. "I won't make this easy for you, Phillipa," he said. And then he was gone.

Mr. Crenshaw went to the kitchen door and turned the dead bolt lever, locking it. "Now we're safe," he said. "No more Honon Miwok *or* Daniel Hernández."

"I'm glad my husband is away," Dr. Paxton said. "He would have been a great support, but I'm afraid his heart couldn't have taken the stress. Why don't we all have a drink of something?"

She gave Mr. Crenshaw a beer, took a glass of wine for herself, and served the boys sodas. They all sat in the living room, sipping, but not talking, in the aftermath of the release of all that tension. The two lamps cast a pleasantly low glow. All's well that end's well, Bob thought.

And then they froze.

There was a noise outside, out back, in the dark. Had Daniel Hernández returned? Phillipa Paxton got to her feet, followed by Martín Crenshaw. Bob clustered together with Pete and Jupe.

Then, sounds that sent fear into Bob's stomach.

Glass breaking, someone reaching in and switching the deadbolt lever, the kitchen door being thrown open.

A growl.

A form leapt into the room, brown and shapeless. Bob, in his confusion, had trouble seeing clearly. What was it?

"I wear the skin of the grizzly bear!" the form screamed.

Whoever it was wore what looked like a rug made of a bearskin on his back. His face was crudely made up. In his hands was a garrote, and Bob finally realized that it was Donovan Jones, the mad Pomo bear-doctor Dasan Coyote, the insane OUTLAW vigilante, the ex-student of Daniel Hernández – who had gotten Dr. Paxton's address from a post Hernández had put on OUTLAW's Facebook page.

He was clearly startled to see a group of people waiting for him, but he ignored all the males, as if they weren't even in the room, and started toward Dr. Paxton, the garrote at the ready.

"Indian killer," he screamed. "Get out of California!"

Bob dove forward. His shoulder hit Donovan Jones behind the kneecaps and he wrapped his arms around the guy's legs. He was followed by Pete who hit him around the waist. Dasan Coyote fell forward into the waiting fists of Martín Crenshaw.

It was all over in a minute. The garrote was swiftly removed from his hands, the bearskin whipped away. On the floor, groaning, lay a pitiful sight. Donovan Jones was wearing a loose pair of cotton pants, a white t-shirt, and sneakers. He moaned and curled into a ball and covered his face with his hands.

"Up you go," Martín Crenshaw said. He grabbed the young man – he was a boy really – under the armpits and dragged him to his feet.

"Don't hit me!" Donovan Jones said. All

the fight had gone out of him.

Jupiter grabbed the other arm and they half-carried him to the kitchen where they sat him in a high-backed wooden chair with a sturdy seat. Pete found a length of clothesline in a utility closet and soon Donovan Jones was secured, hands, chest, and feet fastened to the chair.

This time when Pete asked his father if they should call the Rocky Beach police, there was no disagreement. Bob couldn't believe the Sonoma police had let the guy out in the first place, and he wondered how someone as crazy as Jones had made it all the way from Sonoma to Rocky Beach. He was almost tempted to ask, but decided against it.

Bob shook his head. Jones should be in a hospital, he thought. He was clearly at least partly deranged. Maybe this time the cops would hold on to him. Now that the attack in Sonoma had been followed by a clearly targeted attack hundreds of miles away, Dr. Paxton's safety could not be assured unless this maniacal homicidal stalker was under lock and key. It was Jupiter who made the phone call to Chief Reynolds, and afterwards, they all went back into the kitchen. Dr. Paxton picked up the bearskin Jones had had on his back and looked at it more closely.

"What *is* this?" she said. "This isn't a bearskin. It feels synthetic."

Jones looked at her with what appeared to Bob to be real dismay and shock. "I wouldn't kill a *bear!*" he said. "That's fake fur!"

They left Jones in the kitchen and went back to the living room to await the police. All of them were smiling at what they had just heard.

"Let me sit down," Dr. Paxton said. She slumped onto the sofa, Jupiter on one side of her and Mr. Crenshaw on the other. She looked at one and then the other and started laughing.

"Fake fur, fake bear-doctor, fake Kit Carson letter, fake theory about John Frémont," she said, and started laughing harder.

Soon she was racked with waves of hilarity. Her laughter was infectious, and Mr. Crenshaw started laughing too. Pete and Jupiter smiled and looked at one another, mystified, as Dr. Paxton began to laugh so hard that tears leaked from her eyes and she struggled to breathe. Bob was alarmed. What exactly was so funny? he wondered. It was clear that Dr. Paxton and Mr. Crenshaw were making each other laugh by laughing. Mr. Crenshaw's were deep belly laughs that went on, then stopped, then started again.

Finally, the laughter quieted and Dr. Paxton said, "Just a little bout of hysterics. Nothing to worry about. It's a great release of emotion. You'll understand when you're older."

"Yeah," Mr. Crenshaw said, wiping his eyes. "When you're older."

It wasn't long before they heard a siren, coming toward them, and getting louder. Chief Reynolds was on his way.

"Thanks for everything, Martín," Phillipa Paxton said. "But my real thanks go to the three of you. Thank you, guys. Hurrah for The Three Investigators."

15

A Brobdingnagian Beast

It was three days later, and Pete was due at the Salvage Yard soon. But in the meantime, he was putting in a couple of hours at the Rocky Beach Animal Rescue Center. When he'd arrived, Mr. Munson had told him they had three new rescues – a bald eagle, a coyote, and – to Pete's astonishment – a fully grown but peculiar-looking black bear.

Mr. Munson was the only one there, and he had his hands full, so Pete had helped him feed and water all the other animals before he saw the new arrivals. The eagle had a broken wing and the coyote had been hit by shotgun pellets, but they still looked exactly like the animals they were, Pete thought.

The bear was different. It huddled in a corner of its enclosure staring at Pete with big round sorrowful eyes, and if Mr. Munson hadn't told him it was a bear beforehand, he wouldn't have known what it was.

The luxurious black fur that black bears were known for was completely absent, and its almost hairless skin was flabby – pink and gray and mottled. Little tufts of wiry hair stuck out here and there. Its ears were cupped and stood straight up. Its nose was mostly black but covered with scabs.

"What's wrong with it?" Pete asked.

"It has mange," said Mr. Munson. "A skin disease caused by tiny parasitic mites. The same thing that dogs get sometimes. This case is really bad, though. The people who found him didn't even know what kind of animal he was when they saw him wandering around their neighborhood. His hair may never grow back well enough for us to release him.

"If it doesn't," he added, "he'll just have to stay with us in the Rescue Center – unless we can find a place for him in a rescue facility especially for bears. That would be better, really. Bears are relatively solitary creatures, but no animal wants to be the only one of its kind around."

Mr. Munson went to the office to do some paperwork, leaving Pete sitting on the ground before the bear's enclosure.

"Hi," Pete whispered soothingly. "It's all right, big fella."

The bear looked at him questioningly, slowly got up, walked halfway across the enclosure, and then lay down again. Pete had the sense that that was as close as the two of them were going to get today, but since he didn't think he'd be with Bob and Jupiter for more than an hour or two, he told Mr. Munson he'd come back before dinner to visit the bear again.

Not long afterwards, he was pulling out of the Rescue Center driveway when a car approached, then slowed to a stop beside him. Pete looked up to see Chief Reynolds rolling down the window of his cruiser. The last time he'd seen the Chief had been when he'd arrived at Phillipa Paxton's house to take Dasan Coyote away. Pete took off his helmet to talk.

"Hey, Chief!" Pete called out. "How are you?"

"I was going to ask you the same thing," Chief Reynolds said. "I've also been meaning to call Jupiter to tell him that Donovan Jones's parents have finally gotten involved. I tracked them down, and, with his parents' approval, he's been admitted to a psychiatric hospital."

"That's great," Pete said. "I couldn't believe how lost he seemed when we got him tied to that kitchen chair. He really needs help; you seemed to sense that right away."

"It isn't hard to see when people need help," Chief Reynolds said, smiling. "Will you be playing soccer in the fall?"

Pete nodded enthusiastically. "And baseball in the spring!"

Chief Reynolds grinned. "Let me know if you want to toss a ball around."

He rolled his window up and took off down the street. Pete put his helmet back on and started to pedal toward the Salvage Yard. Chief Reynolds was a great guy, he thought. At a time when a lot of police were in the news for being as bad as the criminals they were supposed to keep their communities safe from, the Chief really stood out.

Of course, policemen – even the good ones – were only a part of what made a community work. The real secret in a place like Rocky Beach was people being willing to listen to one another, instead of trying to shout one another down. The minute people started shouting and not listening, all chance of communication went out the nearest window – and what followed was never pretty.

Fifteen minutes later, Pete was riding his bike through the wrought-iron gates of the Salvage Yard. The door to Easy Three was unlocked and he found Jupe and Bob in Headquarters.

"Hey, guys," he said as he entered.

"Second!" Jupiter said. "We've been waiting for you. We've got a lot to take care of."

"I know," Pete said. "Wrapping up our cases is almost as much work as solving them in the first place."

Bob laughed. "It'll help me a lot if we go over everything and make sure all the loose ends are tied," he said. "Then my work begins. I'm looking forward to having Mr. Crenshaw say, 'I knew you were a villain!'"

"I've been meaning to mention how glad I am that Dr. Paxton had the idea to make sure your father was there with us the other night," Jupiter said. "He looked like a bare-knuckle boxer. First with Hernández and then with Dasan Coyote."

"That's the first time I ever saw my dad do anything like that," Pete said. "He talked to me about it afterwards. He said that you shouldn't use your fists unless you absolutely have to, but when you do, you ought to know how."

"He was perfect," Bob said.

Pete thought so, too, though he hadn't wanted to say so. He'd been bursting with pride for days about the way his father had dealt with Hernández, and later, how cool and in control he'd been when threatened by the Pomo bear-doctor. Pete had always looked up to his father, but now he also felt close to him, and he could tell from the way his father had talked to him that he felt the same way.

Before he and Bob and Jupiter had ever gone up to Sonoma, he'd promised himself he'd get better as an investigator – he'd keep a close watch on Daniel Hernández and get the goods on him, making his father proud. Well, that had certainly been accomplished – though, of course, Bob and Jupe had done more than their fair share.

"Chief Reynolds was terrific, too," Pete said. "I saw him when I was biking over here, and he wanted me to tell you he'd tracked down Donovan Jones's parents, and they've had him admitted to a psychiatric hospital. Also, my father told me that the director of *Bear Valley* fired Hernández.

"All he needed was the photograph Dr. Paxton took of him in her living room with that blood on his jaw – time-stamped with the date she was supposed to be out of town! Mr. Black told him that if he came near the set again, he'd be arrested for trespassing," Pete explained.

"So he's getting it every which way,"

Bob said. "I think we should call Dr. Paxton and see what else has happened on her end. Did your father mention whether she'd be back on the set of the movie?" he asked Pete.

"Dad said she was taking a couple days off," Pete said. "I guess her husband's due back from London this afternoon, and she just wants to take a deep breath before getting back to everything."

"So let's try her at home," Bob said.

Jupiter punched in her number on the Headquarters phone and pressed SPEAKER. The room echoed with the sound of a phone ringing and then was filled with Dr. Paxton's voice.

"Hello," she said. "Phillipa Paxton."

"Dr. Paxton," Jupiter said. "It's Jupiter Jones."

"Jupiter!" she said. "Are Pete and Bob with you?"

"We're here," Pete said.

"Hi, Dr. Paxton," Bob said.

"I don't have a lot of time," Dr. Paxton said. "I have to leave for the airport to pick up my husband. But I was just going to call you to tell you the latest in the Daniel Hernández saga. I sent the Chair of the History Department where Hernández teaches a letter explaining what had happened, together with JPGs of my original Carson letter and Hernández's forgery.

"He called me to tell me he'd handed the file over to the university's Ethics Committee," she added. "As he put it, 'the wheels of academia grind exceedingly slow' – boy, do they ever! – but he's confident that at the end of the investigation, Hernández will lose his job. The forged letter is the reason he got the job in the first place."

"I was talking with my mother," Bob said, "and she mentioned that if he just resigned right away – so there were no formal hearings – he might have a chance of getting another job somewhere else."

"Luckily for college students everywhere, he won't resign," Dr. Paxton said. "He's stubborn, and he seems to think that if he just denies everything, in the end the Ethics Committee will let him stay. Since that anachronism Jupiter found proves beyond a doubt that the letter had to have been written at least three years after its purported date, Hernández's only possible defense is that although it obviously *was* forged, he himself didn't forge it.

"It's at that point that his abilities as a calligrapher become relevant. Not to mention the fact that he was caught red-handed trying to steal the authentic Carson letter in front of five witnesses. I really think he's toast. Also, Richard Black is changing the *Bear Valley* script back to the way it was before Hernández showed up and started making a hash of it."

"That's great news," Jupiter said.

"And even better," Dr. Paxton went on, "Richard contacted OUTLAW and outed Daniel Hernández as Honon Miwok. The group had to deal with the fact that the supposed Miwok Indian agitating for justice and the history professor who benefited from his posts were one and the same man. They felt further betrayed when they learned that Dasan Coyote was an ex-student of his. It looks like OUTLAW will just pack up its outrage and move on to protest something else. But at least they'll leave *Bear Valley* alone."

"Speaking of bears, has Lyle Smith been in touch with you about Jessie Frémont's quilt?" Jupiter asked.

"Yes, I almost forgot!" Dr. Paxton said. "I went to visit him yesterday. Delightful man. I was absolutely knocked out by how beautiful the quilt is, and I agree with your friend Mallory that this is indeed the original. Mr. Smith is going to send it, for authentication, to a museum in San Francisco with a big Frémont collection, and if it confirms what we already know, he'll donate it to the museum. I told him I'd match his generosity, in my own small way. I'm going to donate my Carson letters and anything else in my personal collection that has to do with the Frémonts. Maybe they'll set up a Frémont Room, where everything can be displayed together."

"When the museum opens the exhibition, let's all go!" Bob said.

"It's a date," Phillipa Paxton said. "Richard Black told me that, when filming is over, he's going to give me the replica of the flag quilt that Mallory MacLeod's mother is making, so I'll have my replica after all. Oh, and one last thing. Lyle asked me to thank you for giving him my niece's name, but he's decided he really doesn't need her. Cornelius is getting released from the hospital any day now. Well, I really have to get going. Goodbye for now."

"It's good to talk to you," Jupiter said. "If there's more we can do for you — "

After Jupiter hung up, Pete looked at his two friends, who clearly felt the way he did — thrilled that everything seemed to be working out the way they'd hoped.

"One final thing," Jupiter said. "We promised Branko that if a lead brought us to the quilt we were after, we'd let him know."

"I already took care of that, Jupe," Bob said. "I e-mailed him and told him the whole story. When we go to the exhibition opening, he'll have to come, too. And of course, I'm going to put him into my write-up about the case."

"Good work!" Jupiter said. "And good planning."

"I was thinking," Pete said. "Mr. Small gave us the assayer's scale as a memento of our last case. What about this one?"

Jupiter pointed to one of the bookshelves on the wall of Headquarters. "I think we have our memento already," he said. "Between *Bear Valley* and *Manifest Murder* – and there's a lot between the two! – we have all the memories we'll need. I've been thinking of making a set of bookends to keep the two together."

"That'd be cool!" Pete said.

Actually, Pete was getting a little bit *warm* – he loved Headquarters, but with all the stuff they'd accumulated and with the three of them together, it sometimes seemed a little cramped. "If we don't need to use the phone any more, why don't we go to the workshop and finish talking there?" he suggested.

Soon they were sitting on the old-fashioned green metal chairs they kept in the outside workshop for times like these. The sun dappled the leaves of the trees and a breeze blew through the Salvage Yard. Overhead, a flock of birds wheeled and turned.

"Have you talked to Mallory?" Jupiter asked Bob.

"She came into the library yesterday when I was working and I told her everything," Bob said. "She was very upset about Donovan Jones. When she was in Hernández's office, the Facebook post she saw made it clear that OUTLAW had raised the money to get Dasan Coyote out of jail.

"She kept saying she should have warned us, but I assured her that everything had worked out just fine. Anyway, she was sorry to have missed the big event, but she understood she couldn't be there every time The Three Investigators got the bad guys," Bob said.

"We should be able to give her the immigrant's trunk soon," Jupiter said. "Leif and Magnus have finished making it. In fact, after we're done here, they'd like to take you and the trunk over to the studio of the artist who's going to paint it so you can sign off on her design. At the moment, she's planning to paint vines and flowers, as well as Mallory's name and the year of her arrival in California."

"That sounds great!" said Bob. "It'll be just like the trunk in the bookstore. After Leif and Magnus and I take it to the artist, I can go home and get started on the case report. I've already begun organizing my notes, but I'm having trouble with the title. After *The Mystery of the Abecedarian Academy,* I wanted the second title to have two Bs in it, and so on. Since the two of you seemed to like that idea, I thought I might call this one the mystery of the something-or-other Bear.

"But I'm beginning to worry," he added. "There's the Bear Flag and the Bear Flag Revolt and the commemorative quilt, but there's also the fact that Daniel Hernández used the Miwok name for *bear* as his OUTLAW screen name. Not to mention our friend the Pomo bear-doctor. In a way, there are really too *many* bears floating around."

"Including a real one," Pete said. "This morning at the Rescue Center, I saw a black bear brought in by people who didn't even know what it was. They found it wandering lost in their neighborhood without any fur — all gray and pink, and very scared."

"What's the matter with it?" Bob asked.

"It has mange," Pete said. "And it was all alone and starving."

"That's terrible," Bob said.

"Yes," Jupiter said. "Bears were a real threat to human beings once, but now they need protection from *us*."

"Anyway," Pete went on, "what struck *me* the most about this case was OUTLAW. I can't get out of my mind that day in Sonoma when they were all chanting and punching the air and then suddenly they were through the barricade, like a flood of water bursting through a dam. It was really scary, how they egged each other on."

"Yes," Bob agreed. "A mob has no brain – just animal instinct – and if you let emotion spread through a group of people, it's like unleashing a gigantic, savage beast."

A crow flew down and perched on the edge of a work table, tilting its head and fastening Pete with one bright eye. For a moment he lost the thread of the conversation.

But he paid attention again when Jupiter said, "I like the idea of having the title refer to groups like OUTLAW. After all, without OUTLAW's ignorance about the past, Daniel

Hernández would never have managed to get himself hired as a consultant for Phillipa Paxton's movie, or to provide him with cover for his various schemes."

"I like that idea, too," Bob said. "And *beast* is a good way to describe a mob. But even if I go with the word *beast*, I still don't have an adjective that begins with a 'b'. The best one would be something that means either dangerous or enormous."

"How about Brobdingnagian?" Pete said.

He watched as first Bob and then Jupiter swiveled their heads to look at him in surprise.

"Mallory read this book about a land of giants called Brobdingnag," he explained. "I sometimes don't remember big words, but this time I did! You could call the case *The Mystery of the Brobdingnagian Beast!*"

Bob smiled. "I like that," he said "A lot. And in a way, it's been there all the time – the idea of a strange, shape-shifting creature, dangerous and difficult to pin down – not any specific animal at all, just something large and menacing. The savage part of human beings. The thing that makes them want to stampede and break things or attack the motives or intelligence of people they've never met and know nothing about."

"The day you and I were together at the Animal Rescue Center, Mr. Munson said that people *are* animals – and sometimes a lot more ferocious and wild than all the other animals put together," Pete agreed.

"I think it's a great title," Jupiter said. "Though to *me*, what probably stands out most about this case is the way Hernández and OUTLAW wanted to destroy John Frémont's reputation. Like everyone else, he was a person of his era, but he was also the kind of person a society always needs. An explorer with a curious mind. A man of action who was also a man of science. When people start attacking men and women like that, they're attacking the very people who have made the world they live in."

Pete thought about this for a moment. "That's true, isn't it?" he said. "And you know, that's pretty stupid, because it's a great world, really. And people need to have other people to look up to – people with a prodigious destiny. It was nice of Dr. Paxton to write the inscription in our book the way she did."

"It certainly was," Jupiter said.

They sat for a moment in silence, until Bob said, "Well, I guess I'd better get over to the workshop."

"Yes," Jupiter said. "Leif and Magnus are expecting you."

Pete looked at his watch. "And I promised to get back to the Rescue Center for an hour or so before dinner. What about you, Jupe?"

Jupiter looked a bit embarrassed. "I've got nothing particular to do this evening, but ever since we were in Yosemite and talked about our families, I've been thinking about my mother. The fact that she was supposedly Serbian, but that her name was Amanda Morris. Then going through Jackson and seeing the Serbian church. And now the coincidence of meeting Branko. Of his father saying if I came to Jackson I'd meet other Serbs and he'd make me dance some dance I never heard of."

"The kolo," Bob said. "I can't wait."

"So anyway," Jupiter said. "I think I'm going to look into that a bit."

"That's great, Jupe," Pete said. "I'm glad you're doing that."

"We'll see what comes of it," Jupiter said.

"Does kolo start with a 'c'?" Pete asked. "I can see it now: *The Mystery of the Corlinagenous Colo.*"

Everybody laughed. "That's a great vocabulary you're building, Pete," Bob said. "What does 'corlinagenous' mean?"

"I don't know," Pete said, laughing too. "I just made it up."

They said goodbye. Bob walked toward Leif and Magnus's workshop and Jupiter toward his house, but Pete almost sprinted toward the place he had left his bike. He liked their case wrap-ups, but after an hour or two of sitting and talking, he always had a lot of energy to burn.

He buckled on his helmet, then set off toward the Rescue Center, riding as fast as he could. His legs pumped hard and the wind whipped his face. It felt good to push himself – on the bike but also in the brain – and as he rode, Pete kept thinking about The Three Investigators' recent conversation, particularly the part about John Frémont.

When he and the others had first met Phillipa Paxton, at the movie set in Sonoma, she'd told them all sorts of stuff about Frémont – that he'd made sure that California entered the United States as a free state, not a slave state, that he'd named the Golden Gate Strait and a whole lot of North American flowers. Not to mention leading three big expeditions through the West – two of them guided by Kit Carson.

John Frémont really *had* been an investigator, just as Phillipa Paxton had said, and it was awful to think that a man who'd accomplished so many amazing things during his lifetime could become the focus of so much ignorant rage, by ignorant people. Even though Pete might identify more with Kit Carson than with John Frémont, what Jupiter had said was true. A society needed men like Frémont – an explorer with a curious mind, a man of action who was also a man of science. Which could also be a description of Jupiter.

Not that Jupiter was a man, yet, but he would be someday soon – just the way he and Bob would – and for now, he was Pete's leader. It was pretty awful to imagine that someday a mob of ignorant Yahoos might try to get him too. What the Yahoos had done to Phillipa Paxton at the behest of *their* leader – the lying hypocrite Daniel Hernández! – had really hurt her feelings, and although Jupiter didn't show his feelings all that often, Pete knew he could be hurt, like anyone else. Still, there was no need to worry about that now, Pete thought as he pedaled.

For the moment, the main thing he and

Bob and Jupiter had to worry about was trying to do things they could be proud of afterwards. Dr. Paxton had said there wasn't a state in America that didn't have *something* named after John Frémont, and although it was a different world now − the United States was fully mapped and inhabited − there was still plenty going on that needed investigating.

Pete had never been as good at puzzles as Bob and Jupiter, but he'd always been pretty good both at going after bad guys and exploring and appreciating the world around him, and now he knew that as long as he was part of The Three Investigators, he'd have something important to contribute.

What had Jupiter said back at the motel about human beings wanting to punish people who didn't try hard enough to fit in with the in-group? Right now, Pete couldn't quite remember − but he *did* remember that Jupiter had said that mobs that piled on other people were the reason it was important to protect the rights of individuals over the rights of groups.

When he was younger, Pete had been a fervent Catholic, and he was still religious, in a funny way, so he didn't like to imagine that people could be as bad as they clearly *could* be. But forewarned was forearmed, as his father liked to say.

One day when Pete and his father had been talking, his father had said that history was really about the growth of human knowledge, enlightenment, and wonder, so it was pretty terrible that some schools were hardly teaching it any more. And though Pete himself might prefer to play soccer or baseball or take care of animals – or even baby-sit his younger cousins! – he was glad that Bob and Jupiter, and even Mallory, knew a lot about the past.

Mallory was really pretty cool, Pete thought. When she'd said this case involved a quilt that was supposed to be fake but was ac-tually real, and a letter that was supposed to be real but was actually a fake, she'd been on to something big. And not just about the case, but about life in general. People said, "Seeing is believing," but things weren't always what they appeared to be. You really had to look below the surface to see what was going on.

But happily some things were just what they appeared to be. On the right-hand shoulder of the road ahead of him Pete saw a bright red octagonal sign. He braked and came to a full stop. Then – after looking both ways – he left the sign behind him, and shot forward across the crossroad, pedaling hard.

ABOUT THE AUTHORS

Elizabeth Arthur

Elizabeth was born on November 15, 1953 in New York City. She is the daughter of Robert Arthur, the creator of The Three Investigators series. She was educated at Concord Academy in Concord, Massachusetts, the University of Michigan in Ann Arbor, Michigan, Notre Dame University of Nelson, British Columbia, and the University of Victoria in Victoria, British Columbia.

Before she started working on the New Three Investigators series in December of 2018, Elizabeth spent most of her life writing for adults. *Island Sojourn* – a memoir about building a house on a wilderness island in northern Canada – was published in 1980 by Harper and Row. A second memoir, *Looking For The Klondike Stone*, was published by Knopf in 1992. She is also the author of the novels *Beyond the Mountain, Bad Guys, Binding Spell, Antarctic Navigation,* and *Bring Deeps.*

Elizabeth's writing has received fellowships, grants, and awards from the Bread Loaf Writer's Conference, the Ossabaw Island Project, the Vermont Council on the Arts, and the

Indiana Arts Commission. She twice received fellowships from the National Endowment for the Arts and was the first novelist ever given an Antarctic Artists and Writers Operational Support Grant from the National Science Foundation.

Her novel *Antarctic Navigation* was chosen by the New York *Times* as a Notable Book, received a Critics' Choice Award from the San Francisco *Review of Books*, and was chosen as a Best Book of 1995 by *A Common Reader*. In 1996 the novel received the Ohioana Book Award for Fiction from the Ohioana Library Association.

Elizabeth has also taught creative writing at Miami University in Oxford, Ohio; the University of Cincinnati; and Indiana University/Purdue University of Indianapolis, where she directed the creative writing program. She and Steven Bauer met in 1980 at the Bread Loaf Writer's Conference and have been married since June of 1982.

Steven Bauer

Steven was born on September 10, 1948 in Newark, New Jersey. He was educated at Hanover Park High School in East Hanover, New Jersey, Trinity College in Hartford, Connecticut, and the University of Massachusetts in Amherst, Massachusetts. In 1970 he received a B.A. with Honors in English from Trinity, and in 1975 he received an M.F.A. in English from the University of Massachusetts.

Steven is the author of three books for young people – *Satyrday*, 1980; *The Strange and Wonderful Tale of Robert McDoodle*, 1999; and *A Cat of a Different Color*, 2000. His book of poems *Daylight Savings* was published by Gibbs Smith in 1989 and won the Peregrine Smith Poetry Prize.

Steven's work has received fellowships from the Bread Loaf Writer's Conference and the Fine Arts Work Center in Provincetown, Massachusetts. In addition, he has been given grants and awards from the American Library Association, the Parents' Choice Foundation, the Ossabaw Island Project, the Massachusetts Arts Council, and the Indiana Arts Commission.

From 1979 to 1982, Steven taught literature and creative writing at Colby College in Waterville, Maine. From 1982 to 2009 he taught at Miami University in Oxford, Ohio where he directed the graduate and under-graduate creative writing programs. In 2010 he established Hollow Tree Literary Services, an independent editing business.